From Fairy Balle

Hans Christian Andersen Collection

Thank You

Thank you for purchasing this collection of tales that inspired classical ballets, published by Dance Life Press.

Hans Christian Andersen's stories have been the basis of numerous ballets over the years. There are George Balanchine's *The Steadfast Tin Soldier*, Bronislava Nijinska's *The Ice Maiden*, Arthur Pita's *The Little Match Girl*, Aerin Holt's *The Snow Queen*, John Neumeier's *The Little Mermaid*—and of course the most famous ballet movie of all time, *The Red Shoes*.

Many ballets center on the story of a man who comes in contact with a supernatural creature but they find that they are not able to overcome their differences.

This idea is also prevalent in Andersen's works. We have the little mermaid who is unable to be with the prince, or the tin soldier who falls in love with the ballerina.

Andersen's work has inspired creators to develop numerous ballets based on his stories. This collection includes 6 of Andersen's stories which have inspired classical ballets including *The Snow Queen*, *The Ice Maiden*, *The Little Mermaid*, *The Steadfast Tin Soldier*, *The Little Match Girl*, and *The Red Shoes*.

Thanks so much for your purchase and I hope you enjoy learning more about the stories behind your favorite classical ballets.

Cheers!
Dance Life Press

Table of Contents

The Snow Queen

FIRST STORY. Which Treats of a Mirror and
of the Splinters

Now then, let us begin. When we are at the end of the story, we shall know more than we know now: but to begin.

Once upon a time there was a wicked sprite, indeed he was the most mischievous of all sprites. One day he was in a very good humor, for he had made a mirror with the power of causing all that was good and beautiful when it was reflected therein, to look poor and mean; but that which was good-for-nothing and looked ugly was shown magnified and increased in ugliness.

In this mirror the most beautiful landscapes looked like boiled spinach, and the best persons were turned into frights, or appeared to stand on their heads; their faces were so distorted that they were not to be recognized; and if anyone had a mole, you might be sure that it would be magnified and spread over both nose and mouth.

"That's glorious fun!" said the sprite. If a good thought passed through a man's mind, then a grin was seen in the mirror, and the sprite laughed heartily at his clever discovery. All the little sprites who went to his school—for he kept a sprite school—told each other that a miracle had happened; and that now only, as they thought, it would be possible to see how the world really looked.

They ran about with the mirror; and at last there was not a land or a person who was not represented distorted in the mirror. So then they thought they would fly up to the sky, and have a joke there. The higher they flew with the mirror, the more terribly it grinned: they could hardly hold it fast.

Higher and higher still they flew, nearer and nearer to the stars, when suddenly the mirror shook so terribly with grinning, that it flew out of their hands and fell to the earth, where it was dashed in a hundred million and more pieces. And now it worked much more evil than before; for some of these pieces were hardly so large as a grain of sand, and they flew about in the wide world, and when they got into people's eyes, there they stayed; and then people saw everything perverted, or only had an eye for that which was evil.

This happened because the very smallest bit had the same power which the whole mirror had possessed. Some persons even got a splinter in their heart, and then it made one shudder, for their heart became like a lump of ice. Some of the broken pieces were so large that they were used for windowpanes, through which one could not see one's friends.

Other pieces were put in spectacles; and that was a sad affair when people put on their glasses to see well and rightly. Then the wicked sprite laughed till he almost choked, for all this tickled his fancy. The fine splinters still flew about in the air: and now we shall hear what happened next.

SECOND STORY. A Little Boy and a Little Girl

In a large town, where there are so many houses, and so many people, that there is no roof left for everybody to have a little garden; and where, on this account, most persons are obliged to content themselves with flowers in pots; there lived two little children, who had a garden somewhat larger than a flower-pot. They were not brother and sister; but they cared for each other as much as if they were.

Their parents lived exactly opposite. They inhabited two garrets; and where the roof of the one house joined that of the other, and the gutter ran along the extreme end of it, there was to each house a small window: one needed only to step over the gutter to get from one window to the other.

The children's parents had large wooden boxes there, in which vegetables for the kitchen were planted, and little rose-trees besides: there was a rose in each box, and they grew splendidly. They now thought of placing the boxes across the gutter, so that they nearly reached from one window to the other, and looked just like two walls of flowers.

The tendrils of the peas hung down over the boxes; and the rose-trees shot up long branches, twined round the windows, and then bent towards each other: it was almost like a triumphant arch of foliage and flowers. The boxes were very high, and the children knew that they must not creep over them; so they often obtained permission to get out of the windows to each other, and to sit on their little stools among the roses, where they could play delightfully. In winter there was an end of this pleasure.

The windows were often frozen over; but then they heated copper farthings on the stove, and laid the hot farthing on the windowpane, and then they had a capital peep-hole, quite nicely rounded; and out of each peeped a gentle friendly eye—it was the little boy and the little girl who were looking out.

His name was Kay, hers was Gerda. In summer, with one jump, they could get to each other; but in winter they were obliged first to go down the long stairs, and then up the long stairs again: and out-of-doors there was quite a snow-storm.

"It is the white bees that are swarming," said Kay's old grandmother.

"Do the white bees choose a queen?" asked the little boy; for he knew that the honey-bees always have one.

"Yes," said the grandmother, "she flies where the swarm hangs in the thickest clusters. She is the largest of all; and she can never remain quietly on the earth, but goes up again into the black clouds. Many a winter's night she flies through the streets of the town, and peeps in at the windows; and they then freeze in so wondrous a manner that they look like flowers."

"Yes, I have seen it," said both the children; and so they knew that it was true.

"Can the Snow Queen come in?" said the little girl.

"Only let her come in!" said the little boy. "Then I'd put her on the stove, and she'd melt."

And then his grandmother patted his head and told him other stories.

In the evening, when little Kay was at home, and half undressed, he climbed up on the chair by the window, and peeped out of the little hole. A few snow-flakes were falling, and one, the largest of all, remained lying on the edge of a flower-pot.

The flake of snow grew larger and larger; and at last it was like a young lady, dressed in the finest white gauze, made of a million little flakes like stars. She was so beautiful and delicate, but she was of ice, of dazzling, sparkling ice; yet she lived; her eyes gazed fixedly, like two stars; but there was neither quiet nor repose in them. She nodded towards the window, and beckoned with her hand. The little boy was frightened, and jumped down from the chair; it seemed to him as if, at the same moment, a large bird flew past the window.

The next day it was a sharp frost—and then the spring came; the sun shone, the green leaves appeared, the swallows built their nests, the windows were opened, and the little children again sat in their pretty garden, high up on the leads at the top of the house.

That summer the roses flowered in unwonted beauty. The little girl had learned a hymn, in which there was something about roses; and then she thought of her own flowers; and she sang the verse to the little boy, who then sang it with her:

"The rose in the valley is blooming so sweet,
And angels descend there the children to greet."

And the children held each other by the hand, kissed the roses, looked up at the clear sunshine, and spoke as though they really saw angels there. What lovely summer-days those were! How delightful to be out in the air, near the fresh rose-bushes, that seem as if they would never finish blossoming!

Kay and Gerda looked at the picture-book full of beasts and of birds; and it was then—the clock in the church-tower was just striking five—that Kay said, "Oh! I feel such a sharp pain in my heart; and now something has got into my eye!"

The little girl put her arms around his neck. He winked his eyes; now there was nothing to be seen.

"I think it is out now," said he; but it was not. It was just one of those pieces of glass from the magic mirror that had got into his eye; and poor Kay had got another piece right in his heart. It will soon become like ice. It did not hurt any longer, but there it was.

"What are you crying for?" asked he. "You look so ugly! There's nothing the matter with me. Ah," said he at once, "that rose is cankered! And look, this one is quite crooked! After all, these roses are very ugly! They are just like the box they are planted in!" And then he gave the box a good kick with his foot, and pulled both the roses up.

"What are you doing?" cried the little girl; and as he perceived her fright, he pulled up another rose, got in at the window, and hastened off from dear little Gerda.

Afterwards, when she brought her picture-book, he asked, "What horrid beasts have you there?" And if his grandmother told them stories, he always interrupted her; besides, if he could manage it, he would get behind her, put on her spectacles, and imitate her way of speaking; he copied all her ways, and then everybody laughed at him. He was soon able to imitate the gait and manner of everyone in the street. Everything that was peculiar and displeasing in them—that Kay knew how to imitate: and at such times all the people said, "The boy is certainly very clever!" But it was the glass he had got in his eye; the glass that was sticking in his heart, which made him tease even little Gerda, whose whole soul was devoted to him.

His games now were quite different to what they had formerly been, they were so very knowing. One winter's day, when the flakes of snow were flying about, he spread the skirts of his blue coat, and caught the snow as it fell.

"Look through this glass, Gerda," said he. And every flake seemed larger, and appeared like a magnificent flower, or beautiful star; it was splendid to look at!

"Look, how clever!" said Kay. "That's much more interesting than real flowers! They are as exact as possible; there is not a fault in them, if they did not melt!"

It was not long after this, that Kay came one day with large gloves on, and his little sledge at his back, and bawled right into Gerda's ears, "I have permission to go out into the square where the others are playing"; and off he was in a moment.

There, in the market-place, some of the boldest of the boys used to tie their sledges to the carts as they passed by, and so they were pulled along, and got a good ride. It was so capital! Just as they were in the very height of their amusement, a large sledge passed by: it was painted quite white, and there was someone in it wrapped up in a rough white mantle of fur, with a rough white fur cap on his head. The sledge drove round the square twice, and Kay tied on his sledge as quickly as he could, and off he drove with it.

On they went quicker and quicker into the next street; and the person who drove turned round to Kay, and nodded to him in a friendly manner, just as if they knew each other.

Every time he was going to untie his sledge, the person nodded to him, and then Kay sat quiet; and so on they went till they came outside the gates of the town.

Then the snow began to fall so thickly that the little boy could not see an arm's length before him, but still on he went: when suddenly he let go the string he held in his hand in order to get loose from the sledge, but it was of no use; still the little vehicle rushed on with the quickness of the wind.

He then cried as loud as he could, but no one heard him; the snow drifted and the sledge flew on, and sometimes it gave a jerk as though they were driving over hedges and ditches. He was quite frightened, and he tried to repeat the Lord's Prayer; but all he could do, he was only able to remember the multiplication table.

The snow-flakes grew larger and larger, till at last they looked just like great white fowls. Suddenly they flew on one side; the large sledge stopped, and the person who drove rose up. It was a lady; her cloak and cap were of snow. She was tall and of slender figure, and of a dazzling whiteness. It was the Snow Queen.

"We have travelled fast," said she; "but it is freezingly cold. Come under my bearskin." And she put him in the sledge beside her, wrapped the fur round him, and he felt as though he were sinking in a snow-wreath.

"Are you still cold?" asked she; and then she kissed his forehead. Ah! it was colder than ice; it penetrated to his very heart, which was already almost a frozen lump; it seemed to him as if he were about to die—but a moment more and it was quite congenial to him, and he did not re-mark the cold that was around him.

"My sledge! Do not forget my sledge!" It was the first thing he thought of. It was there tied to one of the white chickens, who flew along with it on his back behind the large sledge. The Snow Queen kissed Kay once more, and then he forgot little Gerda, grandmother, and all whom he had left at his home.

"Now you will have no more kisses," said she, "or else I should kiss you to death!"

Kay looked at her. She was very beautiful; a more clever, or a more lovely countenance he could not fancy to himself; and she no longer appeared of ice as before, when she sat outside the window, and beckoned to him; in his eyes she was perfect, he did not fear her at all, and told her that he could calculate in his head and with fractions, even; that he knew the number of square miles there were in the different countries, and how many inhabitants they contained; and she smiled while he spoke.

It then seemed to him as if what he knew was not enough, and he looked upwards in the large huge empty space above him, and on she flew with him; flew high over the black clouds, while the storm moaned and whistled as though it were singing some old tune.

On they flew over woods and lakes, over seas, and many lands; and beneath them the chilling storm rushed fast, the wolves howled, the snow crackled; above them flew large screaming crows, but higher up appeared the moon, quite large and bright; and it was on it that Kay gazed during the long long winter's night; while by day he slept at the feet of the Snow Queen.

THIRD STORY. Of the Flower-Garden At the Old Woman's Who Understood Witchcraft

But what became of little Gerda when Kay did not return? Where could he be? Nobody knew; nobody could give any intelligence. All the boys knew was, that they had seen him tie his sledge to another large and splendid one, which drove down the street and out of the town. Nobody knew where he was; many sad tears were shed, and little Gerda wept long and bitterly; at last she said he must be dead; that he had been drowned in the river which flowed close to the town. Oh! those were very long and dismal winter evenings!

At last spring came, with its warm sunshine.

"Kay is dead and gone!" said little Gerda.

"That I don't believe," said the Sunshine.

"Kay is dead and gone!" said she to the Swallows.

"That I don't believe," said they: and at last little Gerda did not think so any longer either.

"I'll put on my red shoes," said she, one morning; "Kay has never seen them, and then I'll go down to the river and ask there."

It was quite early; she kissed her old grandmother, who was still asleep, put on her red shoes, and went alone to the river.

"Is it true that you have taken my little playfellow? I will make you a present of my red shoes, if you will give him back to me."

And, as it seemed to her, the blue waves nodded in a strange manner; then she took off her red shoes, the most precious things she possessed, and threw them both into the river. But they fell close to the bank, and the little waves bore them immediately to land; it was as if the stream would not take what was dearest to her; for in reality it had not got little Kay; but Gerda thought that she had not thrown the shoes out far enough, so she clambered into a boat which lay among the rushes, went to the farthest end, and threw out the shoes.

But the boat was not fastened, and the motion which she occasioned, made it drift from the shore. She observed this, and hastened to get back; but before she could do so, the boat was more than a yard from the land, and was gliding quickly onward.

Little Gerda was very frightened, and began to cry; but no one heard her except the sparrows, and they could not carry her to land; but they flew along the bank, and sang as if to comfort her, "Here we are! Here we are!" The boat drifted with the stream, little Gerda sat quite still without shoes, for they were swimming behind the boat, but she could not reach them, because the boat went much faster than they did.

The banks on both sides were beautiful; lovely flowers, venerable trees, and slopes with sheep and cows, but not a human being was to be seen.

"Perhaps the river will carry me to little Kay," said she; and then she grew less sad. She rose, and looked for many hours at the beautiful green banks. Presently she sailed by a large cherry-orchard, where was a little cottage with curious red and blue windows; it was thatched, and before it two wooden soldiers stood sentry, and presented arms when anyone went past.

Gerda called to them, for she thought they were alive; but they, of course, did not answer. She came close to them, for the stream drifted the boat quite near the land.

Gerda called still louder, and an old woman then came out of the cottage, leaning upon a crooked stick. She had a large broad-brimmed hat on, painted with the most splendid flowers.

"Poor little child!" said the old woman. "How did you get upon the large rapid river, to be driven about so in the wide world!" And then the old woman went into the water, caught hold of the boat with her crooked stick, drew it to the bank, and lifted little Gerda out.

And Gerda was so glad to be on dry land again; but she was rather afraid of the strange old woman.

"But come and tell me who you are, and how you came here," said she.

And Gerda told her all; and the old woman shook her head and said, "A-hem! a-hem!" and when Gerda had told her everything, and asked her if she had not seen little Kay, the woman answered that he had not passed there, but he no doubt would come; and she told her not to be cast down, but taste her cherries, and look at her flowers, which were finer than any in a picture-book, each of which could tell a whole story. She then took Gerda by the hand, led her into the little cottage, and locked the door.

The windows were very high up; the glass was red, blue, and green, and the sunlight shone through quite wondrously in all sorts of colors. On the table stood the most exquisite cherries, and Gerda ate as many as she chose, for she had permission to do so. While she was eating, the old woman combed her hair with a golden comb, and her hair curled and shone with a lovely golden color around that sweet little face, which was so round and so like a rose.

"I have often longed for such a dear little girl," said the old woman. "Now you shall see how well we agree together"; and while she combed little Gerda's hair, the child forgot her foster-brother Kay more and more, for the old woman understood magic; but she was no evil being, she only practiced witchcraft a little for her own private amusement, and now she wanted very much to keep little Gerda.

She therefore went out in the garden, stretched out her crooked stick towards the rose-bushes, which, beautifully as they were blowing, all sank into the earth and no one could tell where they had stood. The old woman feared that if Gerda should see the roses, she would then think of her own, would remember little Kay, and run away from her.

She now led Gerda into the flower-garden. Oh, what odor and what loveliness was there! Every flower that one could think of, and of every season, stood there in fullest bloom; no picture-book could be gayer or more beautiful. Gerda jumped for joy, and played till the sun set behind the tall cherry-tree; she then had a pretty bed, with a red silken coverlet filled with blue violets. She fell asleep, and had as pleasant dreams as ever a queen on her wedding-day.

The next morning she went to play with the flowers in the warm sunshine, and thus passed away a day. Gerda knew every flower; and, numerous as they were, it still seemed to Gerda that one was wanting, though she did not know which. One day while she was looking at the hat of the old woman painted with flowers, the most beautiful of them all seemed to her to be a rose. The old woman had forgotten to take it from her hat when she made the others vanish in the earth. But so it is when one's thoughts are not collected.

"What!" said Gerda. "Are there no roses here?" and she ran about amongst the flowerbeds, and looked, and looked, but there was not one to be found. She then sat down and wept; but her hot tears fell just where a rose-bush had sunk; and when her warm tears watered the ground, the tree shot up suddenly as fresh and blooming as when it had been swallowed up. Gerda kissed the roses, thought of her own dear roses at home, and with them of little Kay.

"Oh, how long I have stayed!" said the little girl. "I intended to look for Kay! Don't you know where he is?" she asked of the roses. "Do you think he is dead and gone?"

"Dead he certainly is not," said the Roses. "We have been in the earth where all the dead are, but Kay was not there."

"Many thanks!" said little Gerda; and she went to the other flowers, looked into their cups, and asked, "Don't you know where little Kay is?"

But every flower stood in the sunshine, and dreamed its own fairy tale or its own story: and they all told her very many things, but not one knew anything of Kay.

Well, what did the Tiger-Lily say?

"Hearest thou not the drum? Bum! Bum! Those are the only two tones. Always bum! Bum! Hark to the plaintive song of the old woman, to the call of the priests! The Hindi woman in her long robe stands upon the funeral pile; the flames rise around her and her dead husband, but the Hindi woman thinks on the living one in the surrounding circle; on him whose eyes burn hotter than the flames—on him, the fire of whose eyes pierces her heart more than the flames which soon will burn her body to ashes. Can the heart's flame die in the flame of the funeral pile?"

"I don't understand that at all," said little Gerda.

"That is my story," said the Lily.

What did the Convolvulus say?

"Projecting over a narrow mountain-path there hangs an old feudal castle. Thick evergreens grow on the dilapidated walls, and around the altar, where a lovely maiden is standing: she bends over the railing and looks out upon the rose. No fresher rose hangs on the branches than she; no apple-blossom carried away by the wind is more buoyant! How her silken robe is rustling!

"'Is he not yet come?'"

"Is it Kay that you mean?" asked little Gerda.

"I am speaking about my story—about my dream," answered the Convolvulus.

What did the Snowdrops say?

"Between the trees a long board is hanging—it is a swing. Two little girls are sitting in it, and swing themselves backwards and forwards; their frocks are as white as snow, and long green silk ribands flutter from their bonnets. Their brother, who is older than they are, stands up in the swing; he twines his arms round the cords to hold himself fast, for in one hand he has a little cup, and in the other a clay-pipe.

He is blowing soap-bubbles. The swing moves, and the bubbles float in charming changing colors: the last is still hanging to the end of the pipe, and rocks in the breeze. The swing moves. The little black dog, as light as a soap-bubble, jumps up on his hind legs to try to get into the swing. It moves, the dog falls down, barks, and is angry. They tease him; the bubble bursts! A swing, a bursting bubble—such is my song!"

"What you relate may be very pretty, but you tell it in so melancholy a manner, and do not mention Kay."

What do the Hyacinths say?

"There were once upon a time three sisters, quite transparent, and very beautiful. The robe of the one was red, that of the second blue, and that of the third white. They danced hand in hand beside the calm lake in the clear moonshine. They were not elfin maidens, but mortal children.

A sweet fragrance was smelt, and the maidens vanished in the wood; the fragrance grew stronger—three coffins, and in them three lovely maidens, glided out of the forest and across the lake: the shining glow-worms flew around like little floating lights. Do the dancing maidens sleep, or are they dead? The odor of the flowers says they are corpses; the evening bell tolls for the dead!"

"You make me quite sad," said little Gerda. "I cannot help thinking of the dead maidens. Oh! is little Kay really dead? The Roses have been in the earth, and they say no."

"Ding, dong!" sounded the Hyacinth bells. "We do not toll for little Kay; we do not know him. That is our way of singing, the only one we have."

And Gerda went to the Ranunculuses, that looked forth from among the shining green leaves.

"You are a little bright sun!" said Gerda. "Tell me if you know where I can find my playfellow."

And the Ranunculus shone brightly, and looked again at Gerda. What song could the Ranunculus sing? It was one that said nothing about Kay either.

"In a small court the bright sun was shining in the first days of spring. The beams glided down the white walls of a neighbor's house, and close by the fresh yellow flowers were growing, shining like gold in the warm sun-rays. An old grandmother was sitting in the air; her grand-daughter, the poor and lovely servant just come for a short visit. She knows her grandmother. There was gold, pure virgin gold in that blessed kiss. There, that is my little story," said the Ranunculus.

"My poor old grandmother!" sighed Gerda. "Yes, she is longing for me, no doubt: she is sorrowing for me, as she did for little Kay. But I will soon come home, and then I will bring Kay with me. It is of no use asking the flowers; they only know their own old rhymes, and can tell me nothing." And she tucked up her frock, to enable her to run quicker; but the Narcissus gave her a knock on the leg, just as she was going to jump over it. So she stood still, looked at the long yellow flower, and asked, "You perhaps know something?" and she bent down to the Narcissus. And what did it say?

"I can see myself—I can see myself! Oh, how odorous I am! Up in the little garret there stands, half-dressed, a little Dancer. She stands now on one leg, now on both; she despises the whole world; yet she lives only in imagination. She pours water out of the teapot over a piece of stuff which she holds in her hand; it is the bodice; cleanliness is a fine thing. The white dress is hanging on the hook; it was washed in the teapot, and dried on the roof. She puts it on, ties a saffron-colored kerchief round her neck, and then the gown looks whiter. I can see myself—I can see myself!"

"That's nothing to me," said little Gerda. "That does not concern me." And then off she ran to the further end of the garden.

The gate was locked, but she shook the rusted bolt till it was loosened, and the gate opened; and little Gerda ran off barefooted into the wide world. She looked round her thrice, but no one followed her. At last she could run no longer; she sat down on a large stone, and when she looked about her, she saw that the summer had passed; it was late in the autumn, but that one could not remark in the beauti-ful garden, where there was always sunshine, and where there were flowers the whole year round.

"Dear me, how long I have staid!" said Gerda. "Autumn is come. I must not rest any longer." And she got up to go fur-ther.

Oh, how tender and wearied her little feet were! All around it looked so cold and raw: the long willow-leaves were quite yellow, and the fog dripped from them like water; one leaf fell after the other: the sloes only stood full of fruit, which set one's teeth on edge. Oh, how dark and comfort-less it was in the dreary world!

FOURTH STORY. The Prince and Princess

Gerda was obliged to rest herself again, when, exactly op-posite to her, a large Raven came hopping over the white snow. He had long been looking at Gerda and shaking his head; and now he said, "Caw! Caw!" Good day! Good day! He could not say it better; but he felt a sympathy for the little girl, and asked her where she was going all alone. The word "alone" Gerda understood quite well, and felt how much was expressed by it; so she told the Raven her whole history, and asked if he had not seen Kay.

The Raven nodded very gravely, and said, "It may be—it may be!"

"What, do you really think so?" cried the little girl; and she nearly squeezed the Raven to death, so much did she kiss him.

"Gently, gently," said the Raven. "I think I know; I think that it may be little Kay. But now he has forgotten you for the Princess."

"Does he live with a Princess?" asked Gerda.

"Yes—listen," said the Raven; "but it will be difficult for me to speak your language. If you understand the Raven language I can tell you better."

"No, I have not learnt it," said Gerda; "but my grandmother understands it, and she can speak gibberish too. I wish I had learnt it."

"No matter," said the Raven; "I will tell you as well as I can; however, it will be bad enough." And then he told all he knew.

"In the kingdom where we now are there lives a Princess, who is extraordinarily clever; for she has read all the newspapers in the whole world, and has forgotten them again—so clever is she. She was lately, it is said, sitting on her throne — which is not very amusing after all — when she began humming an old tune, and it was just, 'Oh, why should I not be married?'

'That song is not without its meaning,' said she, and so then she was determined to marry; but she would have a husband who knew how to give an answer when he was spoken to — not one who looked only as if he were a great personage, for that is so tiresome.

She then had all the ladies of the court drummed together; and when they heard her intention, all were very pleased, and said, 'We are very glad to hear it; it is the very thing we were thinking of.' You may believe every word I say," said the Raven; "for I have a tame sweetheart that hops about in the palace quite free, and it was she who told me all this.

"The newspapers appeared forthwith with a border of hearts and the initials of the Princess; and therein you might read that every good-looking young man was at liberty to come to the palace and speak to the Princess; and he who spoke in such wise as showed he felt himself at home there, that one the Princess would choose for her husband.

"Yes, Yes," said the Raven, "you may believe it; it is as true as I am sitting here. People came in crowds; there was a crush and a hurry, but no one was successful either on the first or second day. They could all talk well enough when they were out in the street; but as soon as they came inside the palace gates, and saw the guard richly dressed in silver, and the lackeys in gold on the staircase, and the large illuminated saloons, then they were abashed; and when they stood before the throne on which the Princess was sitting, all they could do was to repeat the last word they had uttered, and to hear it again did not interest her very much.

It was just as if the people within were under a charm, and had fallen into a trance till they came out again into the street; for then—oh, then—they could chatter enough. There was a whole row of them standing from the town-gates to the palace. I was there myself to look," said the Raven. "They grew hungry and thirsty; but from the palace they got nothing whatever, not even a glass of water. Some of the cleverest, it is true, had taken bread and butter with them: but none shared it with his neighbor, for each thought, 'Let him look hungry, and then the Princess won't have him.'"

"But Kay—little Kay," said Gerda, "when did he come? Was he among the number?"

"Patience, patience; we are just come to him. It was on the third day when a little personage without horse or equipage, came marching right boldly up to the palace; his eyes shone like yours, he had beautiful long hair, but his clothes were very shabby."

"That was Kay," cried Gerda, with a voice of delight. "Oh, now I've found him!" and she clapped her hands for joy.

"He had a little knapsack at his back," said the Raven.

"No, that was certainly his sledge," said Gerda; "for when he went away he took his sledge with him."

"That may be," said the Raven; "I did not examine him so minutely; but I know from my tame sweetheart, that when he came into the court-yard of the palace, and saw the body-guard in silver, the lackeys on the staircase, he was not the least abashed; he nodded, and said to them, 'It must be very tiresome to stand on the stairs; for my part, I shall go in.' The saloons were gleaming with lusters—privy councillors and excellencies were walking about barefooted, and wore gold keys; it was enough to make any one feel uncomfortable. His boots creaked, too, so loudly, but still he was not at all afraid."

"That's Kay for certain," said Gerda. "I know he had on new boots; I have heard them creaking in grandmama's room."

"Yes, they creaked," said the Raven. "And on he went boldly up to the Princess, who was sitting on a pearl as large as a spinning-wheel. All the ladies of the court, with their attendants and attendants' attendants, and all the cavaliers, with their gentlemen and gentlemen's gentlemen, stood round; and the nearer they stood to the door, the prouder they looked. It was hardly possible to look at the gentleman's gentleman, so very haughtily did he stand in the doorway."

"It must have been terrible," said little Gerda. "And did Kay get the Princess?"

"Were I not a Raven, I should have taken the Princess myself, although I am promised. It is said he spoke as well as I speak when I talk Raven language; this I learned from my tame sweetheart. He was bold and nicely behaved; he had not come to woo the Princess, but only to hear her wisdom. She pleased him, and he pleased her."

"Yes, yes; for certain that was Kay," said Gerda. "He was so clever; he could reckon fractions in his head. Oh, won't you take me to the palace?"

"That is very easily said," answered the Raven. "But how are we to manage it? I'll speak to my tame sweetheart about it: she must advise us; for so much I must tell you, such a little girl as you are will never get permission to enter."

"Oh, yes I shall," said Gerda; "when Kay hears that I am here, he will come out directly to fetch me."

"Wait for me here on these steps," said the Raven. He moved his head backwards and forwards and flew away.

The evening was closing in when the Raven returned. "Caw —caw!" said he. "She sends you her compliments; and here is a roll for you. She took it out of the kitchen, where there is bread enough. You are hungry, no doubt. It is not possible for you to enter the palace, for you are barefooted: the guards in silver, and the lackeys in gold, would not allow it; but do not cry, you shall come in still. My sweetheart knows a little back stair that leads to the bedchamber, and she knows where she can get the key of it."

And they went into the garden in the large avenue, where one leaf was falling after the other; and when the lights in the palace had all gradually disappeared, the Raven led little Gerda to the back door, which stood half open.

Oh, how Gerda's heart beat with anxiety and longing! It was just as if she had been about to do something wrong; and yet she only wanted to know if little Kay was there. Yes, he must be there. She called to mind his intelligent eyes, and his long hair, so vividly, she could quite see him as he used to laugh when they were sitting under the roses at home. "He will, no doubt, be glad to see you—to hear what a long way you have come for his sake; to know how unhappy all at home were when he did not come back."

Oh, what a fright and a joy it was!

They were now on the stairs. A single lamp was burning there; and on the floor stood the tame Raven, turning her head on every side and looking at Gerda, who bowed as her grandmother had taught her to do.

"My intended has told me so much good of you, my dear young lady," said the tame Raven. "Your tale is very affecting. If you will take the lamp, I will go before. We will go straight on, for we shall meet no one."

"I think there is somebody just behind us," said Gerda; and something rushed past: it was like shadowy figures on the wall; horses with flowing manes and thin legs, huntsmen, ladies and gentlemen on horseback.

"They are only dreams," said the Raven. "They come to fetch the thoughts of the high personages to the chase; 'tis well, for now you can observe them in bed all the better. But let me find, when you enjoy honor and distinction, that you possess a grateful heart."

"Tut! That's not worth talking about," said the Raven of the woods.

They now entered the first saloon, which was of rose-colored satin, with artificial flowers on the wall. Here the dreams were rushing past, but they hastened by so quickly that Gerda could not see the high personages. One hall was more magnificent than the other; one might indeed well be abashed; and at last they came into the bedchamber. The ceiling of the room resembled a large palm-tree with leaves of glass, of costly glass; and in the middle, from a thick golden stem, hung two beds, each of which resembled a lily.

One was white, and in this lay the Princess; the other was red, and it was here that Gerda was to look for little Kay. She bent back one of the red leaves, and saw a brown neck. Oh! that was Kay! She called him quite loud by name, held the lamp towards him—the dreams rushed back again into the chamber—he awoke, turned his head, and—it was not little Kay!

The Prince was only like him about the neck; but he was young and handsome. And out of the white lily leaves the Princess peeped, too, and asked what was the matter. Then little Gerda cried, and told her her whole history, and all that the Ravens had done for her.

"Poor little thing!" said the Prince and the Princess. They praised the Ravens very much, and told them they were not at all angry with them, but they were not to do so again. However, they should have a reward. "Will you fly about here at liberty," asked the Princess; "or would you like to have a fixed appointment as court ravens, with all the broken bits from the kitchen?"

And both the Ravens nodded, and begged for a fixed appointment; for they thought of their old age, and said, "It is a good thing to have a provision for our old days."

And the Prince got up and let Gerda sleep in his bed, and more than this he could not do. She folded her little hands and thought, "How good men and animals are!" and she then fell asleep and slept soundly. All the dreams flew in again, and they now looked like the angels; they drew a little sledge, in which little Kay sat and nodded his head; but the whole was only a dream, and therefore it all vanished as soon as she awoke.

The next day she was dressed from head to foot in silk and velvet. They offered to let her stay at the palace, and lead a happy life; but she begged to have a little carriage with a horse in front, and for a small pair of shoes; then, she said, she would again go forth in the wide world and look for Kay.

Shoes and a muff were given her; she was, too, dressed very nicely; and when she was about to set off, a new carriage stopped before the door. It was of pure gold, and the arms of the Prince and Princess shone like a star upon it; the coachman, the footmen, and the outriders, for outriders were there, too, all wore golden crowns.

The Prince and the Princess assisted her into the carriage themselves, and wished her all success. The Raven of the woods, who was now married, accompanied her for the first three miles. He sat beside Gerda, for he could not bear riding backwards; the other Raven stood in the doorway, and flapped her wings; she could not accompany Gerda, because she suffered from headache since she had had a fixed appointment and ate so much. The carriage was lined inside with sugar-plums, and in the seats were fruits and gingerbread.

"Farewell! Farewell!" cried Prince and Princess; and Gerda wept, and the Raven wept. Thus passed the first miles; and then the Raven bade her farewell, and this was the most painful separation of all. He flew into a tree, and beat his black wings as long as he could see the carriage, that shone from afar like a sunbeam.

FIFTH STORY. The Little Robber Maiden

They drove through the dark wood; but the carriage shone like a torch, and it dazzled the eyes of the robbers, so that they could not bear to look at it.

"'Tis gold! 'Tis gold!" they cried; and they rushed forward, seized the horses, knocked down the little postilion, the coachman, and the servants, and pulled little Gerda out of the carriage.

"How plump, how beautiful she is! She must have been fed on nut-kernels," said the old female robber, who had a long, scrubby beard, and bushy eyebrows that hung down over her eyes. "She is as good as a fatted lamb! How nice she will be!" And then she drew out a knife, the blade of which shone so that it was quite dreadful to behold.

"Oh!" cried the woman at the same moment. She had been bitten in the ear by her own little daughter, who hung at her back; and who was so wild and unmanageable, that it was quite amusing to see her. "You naughty child!" said the mother: and now she had not time to kill Gerda.

"She shall play with me," said the little robber child. "She shall give me her muff, and her pretty frock; she shall sleep in my bed!" And then she gave her mother another bite, so that she jumped, and ran round with the pain; and the Robbers laughed, and said, "Look, how she is dancing with the little one!"

"I will go into the carriage," said the little robber maiden; and she would have her will, for she was very spoiled and very headstrong. She and Gerda got in; and then away they drove over the stumps of felled trees, deeper and deeper into the woods. The little robber maiden was as tall as Gerda, but stronger, broader-shouldered, and of dark complexion; her eyes were quite black; they looked almost melancholy. She embraced little Gerda, and said, "They shall not kill you as long as I am not displeased with you. You are, doubtless, a Princess?"

"No," said little Gerda; who then related all that had happened to her, and how much she cared about little Kay.

The little robber maiden looked at her with a serious air, nodded her head slightly, and said, "They shall not kill you, even if I am angry with you: then I will do it myself"; and she dried Gerda's eyes, and put both her hands in the handsome muff, which was so soft and warm.

At length the carriage stopped. They were in the midst of the court-yard of a robber's castle. It was full of cracks from top to bottom; and out of the openings magpies and rooks were flying; and the great bull-dogs, each of which looked as if he could swallow a man, jumped up, but they did not bark, for that was forbidden.

In the midst of the large, old, smoking hall burnt a great fire on the stone floor. The smoke disappeared under the stones, and had to seek its own egress. In an immense caldron soup was boiling; and rabbits and hares were being roasted on a spit.

"You shall sleep with me to-night, with all my animals," said the little robber maiden. They had something to eat and drink; and then went into a corner, where straw and carpets were lying. Beside them, on laths and perches, sat nearly a hundred pigeons, all asleep, seemingly; but yet they moved a little when the robber maiden came. "They are all mine," said she, at the same time seizing one that was next to her by the legs and shaking it so that its wings fluttered.

"Kiss it," cried the little girl, and flung the pigeon in Gerda's face. "Up there is the rabble of the wood," continued she, pointing to several laths which were fastened before a hole high up in the wall; "that's the rabble; they would all fly away immediately, if they were not well fastened in. And here is my dear old Bac"; and she laid hold of the horns of a reindeer, that had a bright copper ring round its neck, and was tethered to the spot.

"We are obliged to lock this fellow in too, or he would make his escape. Every evening I tickle his neck with my sharp knife; he is so frightened at it!" and the little girl drew forth a long knife, from a crack in the wall, and let it glide over the Reindeer's neck. The poor animal kicked; the girl laughed, and pulled Gerda into bed with her.

"Do you intend to keep your knife while you sleep?" asked Gerda; looking at it rather fearfully.

"I always sleep with the knife," said the little robber maiden. "There is no knowing what may happen. But tell me now, once more, all about little Kay; and why you have started off in the wide world alone." And Gerda related all, from the very beginning: the Wood-pigeons cooed above in their cage, and the others slept.

The little robber maiden wound her arm round Gerda's neck, held the knife in the other hand, and snored so loud that everybody could hear her; but Gerda could not close her eyes, for she did not know whether she was to live or die. The robbers sat round the fire, sang and drank; and the old female robber jumped about so, that it was quite dreadful for Gerda to see her.

Then the Wood-pigeons said, "Coo! Coo! We have seen little Kay! A white hen carries his sledge; he himself sat in the carriage of the Snow Queen, who passed here, down just over the wood, as we lay in our nest. She blew upon us young ones; and all died except we two. Coo! Coo!"

"What is that you say up there?" cried little Gerda. "Where did the Snow Queen go to? Do you know anything about it?"

"She is no doubt gone to Lapland; for there is always snow and ice there. Only ask the Reindeer, who is tethered there."

"Ice and snow is there! There it is, glorious and beautiful!" said the Reindeer. "One can spring about in the large shining valleys! The Snow Queen has her summer-tent there; but her fixed abode is high up towards the North Pole, on the Island called Spitzbergen."

"Oh, Kay! Poor little Kay!" sighed Gerda.

"Do you choose to be quiet?" said the robber maiden. "If you don't, I shall make you."

In the morning Gerda told her all that the Wood-pigeons had said; and the little maiden looked very serious, but she nodded her head, and said, "That's no matter—that's no matter. Do you know where Lapland lies!" she asked of the Reindeer.

"Who should know better than I?" said the animal; and his eyes rolled in his head. "I was born and bred there—there I leapt about on the fields of snow."

"Listen," said the robber maiden to Gerda. "You see that the men are gone; but my mother is still here, and will remain. However, towards morning she takes a draught out of the large flask, and then she sleeps a little: then I will do something for you." She now jumped out of bed, flew to her mother; with her arms round her neck, and pulling her by the beard, said, "Good morrow, my own sweet nanny-goat of a mother." And her mother took hold of her nose, and pinched it till it was red and blue; but this was all done out of pure love.

When the mother had taken a sup at her flask, and was having a nap, the little robber maiden went to the Reindeer, and said, "I should very much like to give you still many a tickling with the sharp knife, for then you are so amusing; however, I will untether you, and help you out, so that you may go back to Lapland. But you must make good use of your legs; and take this little girl for me to the palace of the Snow Queen, where her playfellow is. You have heard, I suppose, all she said; for she spoke loud enough, and you were listening."

The Reindeer gave a bound for joy. The robber maiden lifted up little Gerda, and took the precaution to bind her fast on the Reindeer's back; she even gave her a small cushion to sit on. "Here are your worsted leggings, for it will be cold; but the muff I shall keep for myself, for it is so very pretty. But I do not wish you to be cold. Here is a pair of lined gloves of my mother's; they just reach up to your elbow. On with them! Now you look about the hands just like my ugly old mother!"

And Gerda wept for joy.

"I can't bear to see you fretting," said the little robber maiden. "This is just the time when you ought to look pleased. Here are two loaves and a ham for you, so that you won't starve." The bread and the meat were fastened to the

Reindeer's back; the little maiden opened the door, called in all the dogs, and then with her knife cut the rope that fastened the animal, and said to him, "Now, off with you; but take good care of the little girl!"

And Gerda stretched out her hands with the large wadded gloves towards the robber maiden, and said, "Farewell!" and the Reindeer flew on over bush and bramble through the great wood, over moor and heath, as fast as he could go.

"Ddsa! Ddsa!" was heard in the sky. It was just as if somebody was sneezing.

"These are my old northern-lights," said the Reindeer, "look how they gleam!" And on he now sped still quicker—day and night on he went: the loaves were consumed, and the ham too; and now they were in Lapland.

SIXTH STORY. The Lapland Woman and the Finland Woman

Suddenly they stopped before a little house, which looked very miserable. The roof reached to the ground; and the door was so low, that the family were obliged to creep upon their stomachs when they went in or out. Nobody was at home except an old Lapland woman, who was dressing fish by the light of an oil lamp. And the Reindeer told her the whole of Gerda's history, but first of all his own; for that seemed to him of much greater importance. Gerda was so chilled that she could not speak.

"Poor thing," said the Lapland woman, "you have far to run still. You have more than a hundred miles to go before you get to Finland; there the Snow Queen has her country-house, and burns blue lights every evening. I will give you a few words from me, which I will write on a dried haber-dine, for paper I have none; this you can take with you to the Finland woman, and she will be able to give you more information than I can."

When Gerda had warmed herself, and had eaten and drunk, the Lapland woman wrote a few words on a dried haber-dine, begged Gerda to take care of them, put her on the Reindeer, bound her fast, and away sprang the animal. "Ddsa! Ddsa!" was again heard in the air; the most charm-ing blue lights burned the whole night in the sky, and at last they came to Finland. They knocked at the chimney of the Finland woman; for as to a door, she had none.

There was such a heat inside that the Finland woman her-self went about almost naked. She was diminutive and dirty. She immediately loosened little Gerda's clothes, pulled off her thick gloves and boots; for otherwise the heat would have been too great—and after laying a piece of ice on the Reindeer's head, read what was written on the fish-skin. She read it three times: she then knew it by heart; so she put the fish into the cupboard—for it might very well be eaten, and she never threw anything away.

Then the Reindeer related his own story first, and after-wards that of little Gerda; and the Finland woman winked her eyes, but said nothing.

"You are so clever," said the Reindeer; "you can, I know, twist all the winds of the world together in a knot. If the seaman loosens one knot, then he has a good wind; if a second, then it blows pretty stiffly; if he undoes the third and fourth, then it rages so that the forests are upturned. Will you give the little maiden a potion, that she may possess the strength of twelve men, and vanquish the Snow Queen?"

"The strength of twelve men!" said the Finland woman. "Much good that would be!" Then she went to a cupboard, and drew out a large skin rolled up. When she had unrolled it, strange characters were to be seen written thereon; and the Finland woman read at such a rate that the perspiration trickled down her forehead.

But the Reindeer begged so hard for little Gerda, and Gerda looked so imploringly with tearful eyes at the Finland woman, that she winked, and drew the Reindeer aside into a corner, where they whispered together, while the animal got some fresh ice put on his head.

"'Tis true little Kay is at the Snow Queen's, and finds everything there quite to his taste; and he thinks it the very best place in the world; but the reason of that is, he has a splinter of glass in his eye, and in his heart. These must be got out first; otherwise he will never go back to mankind, and the Snow Queen will retain her power over him."

"But can you give little Gerda nothing to take which will endue her with power over the whole?"

"I can give her no more power than what she has already. Don't you see how great it is? Don't you see how men and animals are forced to serve her; how well she gets through the world barefooted? She must not hear of her power from us; that power lies in her heart, because she is a sweet and innocent child! If she cannot get to the Snow Queen by herself, and rid little Kay of the glass, we cannot help her.

Two miles hence the garden of the Snow Queen begins; thither you may carry the little girl. Set her down by the large bush with red berries, standing in the snow; don't stay talking, but hasten back as fast as possible." And now the Finland woman placed little Gerda on the Reindeer's back, and off he ran with all imaginable speed.

"Oh! I have not got my boots! I have not brought my gloves!" cried little Gerda. She remarked she was without them from the cutting frost; but the Reindeer dared not stand still; on he ran till he came to the great bush with the red berries, and there he set Gerda down, kissed her mouth, while large bright tears flowed from the animal's eyes, and then back he went as fast as possible. There stood poor Gerda now, without shoes or gloves, in the very middle of dreadful icy Finland.

She ran on as fast as she could. There then came a whole regiment of snow-flakes, but they did not fall from above, and they were quite bright and shining from the Aurora Borealis. The flakes ran along the ground, and the nearer they came the larger they grew. Gerda well remembered how large and strange the snow-flakes appeared when she once saw them through a magnifying-glass; but now they were large and terrific in another manner—they were all alive. They were the outposts of the Snow Queen.

They had the most wondrous shapes; some looked like large ugly porcupines; others like snakes knotted together, with their heads sticking out; and others, again, like small fat bears, with the hair standing on end: all were of dazzling whiteness—all were living snow-flakes.

Little Gerda repeated the Lord's Prayer. The cold was so intense that she could see her own breath, which came like smoke out of her mouth. It grew thicker and thicker, and took the form of little angels, that grew more and more when they touched the earth. All had helms on their heads, and lances and shields in their hands; they increased in numbers; and when Gerda had finished the Lord's Prayer, she was surrounded by a whole legion.

They thrust at the horrid snow-flakes with their spears, so that they flew into a thousand pieces; and little Gerda walked on bravely and in security. The angels patted her hands and feet; and then she felt the cold less, and went on quickly towards the palace of the Snow Queen.

But now we shall see how Kay fared. He never thought of Gerda, and least of all that she was standing before the palace.

SEVENTH STORY. What Took Place in the Palace of the Snow Queen, and What Happened Afterward

The walls of the palace were of driving snow, and the windows and doors of cutting winds. There were more than a hundred halls there, according as the snow was driven by the winds. The largest was many miles in extent; all were lighted up by the powerful Aurora Borealis, and all were so large, so empty, so icy cold, and so resplendent! Mirth never reigned there; there was never even a little bear-ball, with the storm for music, while the polar bears went on their hind legs and showed off their steps. Never a little tea-party of white young lady foxes; vast, cold, and empty were the halls of the Snow Queen.

The northern-lights shone with such precision that one could tell exactly when they were at their highest or lowest degree of brightness. In the middle of the empty, endless hall of snow, was a frozen lake; it was cracked in a thousand pieces, but each piece was so like the other, that it seemed the work of a cunning artificer. In the middle of this lake sat the Snow Queen when she was at home; and then she said she was sitting in the Mirror of Understanding, and that this was the only one and the best thing in the world.

Little Kay was quite blue, yes nearly black with cold; but he did not observe it, for she had kissed away all feeling of cold from his body, and his heart was a lump of ice. He was dragging along some pointed flat pieces of ice, which he laid together in all possible ways, for he wanted to make something with them; just as we have little flat pieces of wood to make geometrical figures with, called the Chinese Puzzle.

Kay made all sorts of figures, the most complicated, for it was an ice-puzzle for the understanding. In his eyes the figures were extraordinarily beautiful, and of the utmost importance; for the bit of glass which was in his eye caused this. He found whole figures which represented a written word; but he never could manage to represent just the word he wanted—that word was "eternity"; and the Snow Queen had said, "If you can discover that figure, you shall be your own master, and I will make you a present of the whole world and a pair of new skates." But he could not find it out.

"I am going now to warm lands," said the Snow Queen. "I must have a look down into the black caldrons." It was the volcanoes Vesuvius and Etna that she meant. "I will just give them a coating of white, for that is as it ought to be; besides, it is good for the oranges and the grapes." And then away she flew, and Kay sat quite alone in the empty halls of ice that were miles long, and looked at the blocks of ice, and thought and thought till his skull was almost cracked. There he sat quite benumbed and motionless; one would have imagined he was frozen to death.

Suddenly little Gerda stepped through the great portal into the palace. The gate was formed of cutting winds; but Gerda repeated her evening prayer, and the winds were laid as though they slept; and the little maiden entered the vast, empty, cold halls. There she beheld Kay: she recognized him, flew to embrace him, and cried out, her arms firmly holding him the while, "Kay, sweet little Kay! Have I then found you at last?"

But he sat quite still, benumbed and cold. Then little Gerda shed burning tears; and they fell on his bosom, they penetrated to his heart, they thawed the lumps of ice, and consumed the splinters of the looking-glass; he looked at her, and she sang the hymn:

> *"The rose in the valley is blooming so sweet,*
> *And angels descend there the children to greet."*

Hereupon Kay burst into tears; he wept so much that the splinter rolled out of his eye, and he recognized her, and shouted, "Gerda, sweet little Gerda! Where have you been so long? And where have I been?" He looked round him. "How cold it is here!" said he. "How empty and cold!" And he held fast by Gerda, who laughed and wept for joy. It was so beautiful, that even the blocks of ice danced about for joy; and when they were tired and laid themselves down, they formed exactly the letters which the Snow Queen had told him to find out; so now he was his own master, and he would have the whole world and a pair of new skates into the bargain.

Gerda kissed his cheeks, and they grew quite blooming; she kissed his eyes, and they shone like her own; she kissed his hands and feet, and he was again well and merry. The Snow Queen might come back as soon as she liked; there stood his discharge written in resplendent masses of ice.

They took each other by the hand, and wandered forth out of the large hall; they talked of their old grandmother, and of the roses upon the roof; and wherever they went, the winds ceased raging, and the sun burst forth. And when they reached the bush with the red berries, they found the Reindeer waiting for them.

He had brought another, a young one, with him, whose udder was filled with milk, which he gave to the little ones, and kissed their lips. They then carried Kay and Gerda— first to the Finland woman, where they warmed themselves in the warm room, and learned what they were to do on their journey home; and they went to the Lapland woman, who made some new clothes for them and repaired their sledges.

The Reindeer and the young hind leaped along beside them, and accompanied them to the boundary of the country. Here the first vegetation peeped forth; here Kay and Gerda took leave of the Lapland woman. "Farewell! Farewell!" they all said. And the first green buds appeared, the first little birds began to chirrup; and out of the wood came, riding on a magnificent horse, which Gerda knew (it was one of the leaders in the golden carriage), a young damsel with a bright-red cap on her head, and armed with pistols. It was the little robber maiden, who, tired of being at home, had determined to make a journey to the north; and afterwards in another direction, if that did not please her. She recognized Gerda immediately, and Gerda knew her too. It was a joyful meeting.

"You are a fine fellow for tramping about," said she to little Kay; "I should like to know, faith, if you deserve that one should run from one end of the world to the other for your sake?"

But Gerda patted her cheeks, and inquired for the Prince and Princess.

"They are gone abroad," said the other.

"But the Raven?" asked little Gerda.

"Oh! The Raven is dead," she answered. "His tame sweet-heart is a widow, and wears a bit of black worsted round her leg; she laments most piteously, but it's all mere talk and stuff! Now tell me what you've been doing and how you managed to catch him."

And Gerda and Kay both told their story.

And "Schnipp-schnapp-schnurre-basselurre," said the robber maiden; and she took the hands of each, and promised that if she should some day pass through the town where they lived, she would come and visit them; and then away she rode. Kay and Gerda took each other's hand: it was lovely spring weather, with abundance of flowers and of verdure. The church-bells rang, and the children recognized the high towers, and the large town; it was that in which they dwelt. They entered and hastened up to their grand-mother's room, where everything was standing as formerly.

The clock said "tick! tack!" and the finger moved round; but as they entered, they remarked that they were now grown up. The roses on the leads hung blooming in at the open window; there stood the little children's chairs, and Kay and Gerda sat down on them, holding each other by the hand; they both had forgotten the cold empty splendor of the Snow Queen, as though it had been a dream. The grandmother sat in the bright sunshine, and read aloud from the Bible: "Unless ye become as little children, ye cannot enter the kingdom of heaven."

And Kay and Gerda looked in each other's eyes, and all at once they understood the old hymn:

"The rose in the valley is blooming so sweet, And angels descend there the children to greet."

There sat the two grown-up persons; grown-up, and yet children; children at least in heart; and it was summer-time; summer, glorious summer!

The Steadfast Tin Soldier

There were once five and twenty tin soldiers. They were brothers, for they had all been made out of the same old tin spoon. They all shouldered their bayonets, held themselves upright, and looked straight before them. Their uniforms were very smart-looking—red and blue—and very splendid.

The first thing they heard in the world, when the lid was taken off the box in which they lay, was the words "Tin soldiers!" These words were spoken by a little boy, who clapped his hands for joy. The soldiers had been given him because it was his birthday, and now he was putting them out upon the table.

Each was exactly like the rest to a hair, except one who had but one leg. He had been cast last of all, and there had not been quite enough tin to finish him; but he stood as firmly upon his one leg as the others upon their two, and it was he whose fortunes became so remarkable.

On the table where the tin soldiers had been set up were several other toys, but the one that attracted most attention was a pretty little paper castle. Through its tiny windows one could see straight into the hall. In front of the castle stood little trees, clustering round a small mirror which was meant to represent a transparent lake. Swans of wax swam upon its surface, and it reflected back their images.

All this was very pretty, but prettiest of all was a little lady who stood at the castle's open door. She too was cut out of paper, but she wore a frock of the clearest gauze and a narrow blue ribbon over her shoulders, like a scarf, and in the middle of the ribbon was placed a shining tinsel rose. The little lady stretched out both her arms, for she was a dancer, and then she lifted one leg so high that the Soldier quite lost sight of it. He thought that, like himself, she had but one leg.

"That would be just the wife for me," thought he, "if she were not too grand. But she lives in a castle, while I have only a box, and there are five and twenty of us in that. It would be no place for a lady. Still, I must try to make her acquaintance." A snuffbox happened to be upon the table and he lay down at full length behind it, and here he could easily watch the dainty little lady, who still remained standing on one leg without losing her balance.

When the evening came all the other tin soldiers were put away in their box, and the people in the house went to bed. Now the playthings began to play in their turn. They visited, fought battles, and gave balls. The tin soldiers rattled in the box, for they wished to join the rest, but they could not lift the lid.

The nutcrackers turned somersaults, and the pencil jumped about in a most amusing way. There was such a din that the canary woke and began to speak—and in verse, too. The only ones who did not move from their places were the Tin Soldier and the Lady Dancer. She stood on tiptoe with outstretched arms, and he was just as persevering on his one leg; he never once turned away his eyes from her.

Twelve o'clock struck—crash! up sprang the lid of the snuffbox. There was no snuff in it, but a little black goblin. You see it was not a real snuffbox, but a jack-in-the-box.

"Tin Soldier," said the Goblin, "keep thine eyes to thyself. Gaze not at what does not concern thee!"

But the Tin Soldier pretended not to hear.

"Only wait, then, till to-morrow," remarked the Goblin.

Next morning, when the children got up, the Tin Soldier was placed on the window sill, and, whether it was the Goblin or the wind that did it, all at once the window flew open and the Tin Soldier fell head foremost from the third story to the street below. It was a tremendous fall! Over and over he turned in the air, till at last he rested, his cap and bayonet sticking fast between the paving stones, while his one leg stood upright in the air.

The maidservant and the little boy came down at once to look for him, but, though they nearly trod upon him, they could not manage to find him. If the Soldier had but once called "Here am I!" they might easily enough have heard him, but he did not think it becoming to cry out for help, being in uniform.

It now began to rain; faster and faster fell the drops, until there was a heavy shower; and when it was over, two street boys came by.

"Look you," said one, "there lies a tin soldier. He must come out and sail in a boat."

So they made a boat out of an old newspaper and put the Tin Soldier in the middle of it, and away he sailed down the gutter, while the boys ran along by his side, clapping their hands.

Goodness! How the waves rocked that paper boat, and how fast the stream ran! The Tin Soldier became quite giddy, the boat veered round so quickly; still he moved not a muscle, but looked straight before him and held his bayonet tightly.

All at once the boat passed into a drain, and it became as dark as his own old home in the box. "Where am I going now?" thought he. "Yes, to be sure, it is all that Goblin's doing. Ah! if the little lady were but sailing with me in the boat, I would not care if it were twice as dark."

Just then a great water rat, that lived under the drain, darted suddenly out.

"Have you a passport?" asked the rat. "Where is your passport?"

But the Tin Soldier kept silence and only held his bayonet with a firmer grasp.

The boat sailed on, but the rat followed. Whew! how he gnashed his teeth and cried to the sticks and straws: "Stop him! stop him! He hasn't paid toll! He hasn't shown his passport!"

But the stream grew stronger and stronger. Already the Tin Soldier could see daylight at the point where the tunnel ended; but at the same time he heard a rushing, roaring noise, at which a bolder man might have trembled. Think! just where the tunnel ended, the drain widened into a great sheet that fell into the mouth of a sewer. It was as perilous a situation for the Soldier as sailing down a mighty waterfall would be for us.

He was now so near it that he could not stop. The boat dashed on, and the Tin Soldier held himself so well that no one might say of him that he so much as winked an eye. Three or four times the boat whirled round and round; it was full of water to the brim and must certainly sink.

The Tin Soldier stood up to his neck in water; deeper and deeper sank the boat, softer and softer grew the paper; and now the water closed over the Soldier's head. He thought of the pretty little dancer whom he should never see again, and in his ears rang the words of the song:

> *Wild adventure, mortal danger,*
> *Be thy portion, valiant stranger.*

The paper boat parted in the middle, and the Soldier was about to sink, when he was swallowed by a great fish.

Oh, how dark it was! Darker even than in the drain, and so narrow; but the Tin Soldier retained his courage; there he lay at full length, shouldering his bayonet as before.

To and fro swam the fish, turning and twisting and making the strangest movements, till at last he became perfectly still.

Something like a flash of daylight passed through him, and a voice said, "Tin Soldier!"

The fish had been caught, taken to market, sold and bought, and taken to the kitchen, where the cook had cut him with a large knife. She seized the Tin Soldier between her finger and thumb and took him to the room where the family sat, and where all were eager to see the celebrated man who had traveled in the maw of a fish; but the Tin Soldier remained unmoved. He was not at all proud.

They set him upon the table there. But how could so curious a thing happen? The Soldier was in the very same room in which he had been before. He saw the same children, the same toys stood upon the table, and among them the pretty dancing maiden, who still stood upon one leg. She too was steadfast. That touched the Tin Soldier's heart. He could have wept tin tears, but that would not have been proper.

He looked at her and she looked at him, but neither spoke a word.

And now one of the little boys took the Tin Soldier and threw him into the stove. He gave no reason for doing so, but no doubt the Goblin in the snuffbox had something to do with it.

The Tin Soldier stood now in a blaze of red light. The heat he felt was terrible, but whether it proceeded from the fire or from the love in his heart, he did not know. He saw that the colors were quite gone from his uniform, but whether that had happened on the journey or had been caused by grief, no one could say. He looked at the little lady, she looked at him, and he felt himself melting; still he stood firm as ever, with his bayonet on his shoulder.

Then suddenly the door flew open; the wind caught the Dancer, and she flew straight into the stove to the Tin Soldier, flashed up in a flame, and was gone! The Tin Soldier melted into a lump; and in the ashes the maid found him next day, in the shape of a little tin heart, while of the Dancer nothing remained save the tinsel rose, and that was burned as black as a coal.

The Little Mermaid

Far out in the ocean, where the water is as blue as the prettiest cornflower and as clear as crystal, it is very, very deep; so deep, indeed, that no cable could sound it, and many church steeples, piled one upon another, would not reach from the ground beneath to the surface of the water above. There dwell the Sea King and his subjects.

We must not imagine that there is nothing at the bottom of the sea but bare yellow sand. No, indeed, for on this sand grow the strangest flowers and plants, the leaves and stems of which are so pliant that the slightest agitation of the water causes them to stir as if they had life. Fishes, both large and small, glide between the branches as birds fly among the trees here upon land.

In the deepest spot of all stands the castle of the Sea King. Its walls are built of coral, and the long Gothic windows are of the clearest amber. The roof is formed of shells that open and close as the water flows over them. Their appearance is very beautiful, for in each lies a glittering pearl which would be fit for the diadem of a queen.

The Sea King had been a widower for many years, and his aged mother kept house for him. She was a very sensible woman, but exceedingly proud of her high birth, and on that account wore twelve oysters on her tail, while others of high rank were only allowed to wear six.

She was, however, deserving of very great praise, especially for her care of the little sea princesses, her six granddaughters. They were beautiful children, but the youngest was the prettiest of them all. Her skin was as clear and delicate as a rose leaf, and her eyes as blue as the deepest sea;

but, like all the others, she had no feet and her body ended in a fish's tail.

All day long they played in the great halls of the castle or among the living flowers that grew out of the walls. The large amber windows were open, and the fish swam in, just as the swallows fly into our houses when we open the windows; only the fishes swam up to the princesses, ate out of their hands, and allowed themselves to be stroked.

Outside the castle there was a beautiful garden, in which grew bright-red and dark-blue flowers, and blossoms like flames of fire; the fruit glittered like gold, and the leaves and stems waved to and fro continually. The earth itself was the finest sand, but blue as the flame of burning sulphur. Over everything lay a peculiar blue radiance, as if the blue sky were everywhere, above and below, instead of the dark depths of the sea. In calm weather the sun could be seen, looking like a reddish-purple flower with light streaming from the calyx.

Each of the young princesses had a little plot of ground in the garden, where she might dig and plant as she pleased. One arranged her flower bed in the form of a whale; another preferred to make hers like the figure of a little mermaid; while the youngest child made hers round, like the sun, and in it grew flowers as red as his rays at sunset.

She was a strange child, quiet and thoughtful. While her sisters showed delight at the wonderful things which they obtained from the wrecks of vessels, she cared only for her pretty flowers, red like the sun, and a beautiful marble statue. It was the representation of a handsome boy, carved out of pure white stone, which had fallen to the bottom of the sea from a wreck.

She planted by the statue a rose-colored weeping willow. It grew rapidly and soon hung its fresh branches over the statue, almost down to the blue sands. The shadows had the color of violet and waved to and fro like the branches, so that it seemed as if the crown of the tree and the root were at play, trying to kiss each other.

Nothing gave her so much pleasure as to hear about the world above the sea. She made her old grandmother tell her all she knew of the ships and of the towns, the people and the animals. To her it seemed most wonderful and beautiful to hear that the flowers of the land had fragrance, while those below the sea had none; that the trees of the forest were green; and that the fishes among the trees could sing so sweetly that it was a pleasure to listen to them. Her grandmother called the birds fishes, or the little mermaid would not have understood what was meant, for she had never seen birds.

"When you have reached your fifteenth year," said the grandmother, "you will have permission to rise up out of the sea and sit on the rocks in the moonlight, while the great ships go sailing by. Then you will see both forests and towns."

In the following year, one of the sisters would be fifteen, but as each was a year younger than the other, the youngest would have to wait five years before her turn came to rise up from the bottom of the ocean to see the earth as we do. However, each promised to tell the others what she saw on her first visit and what she thought was most beautiful. Their grandmother could not tell them enough—there were so many things about which they wanted to know.

None of them longed so much for her turn to come as the youngest—she who had the longest time to wait and who was so quiet and thoughtful. Many nights she stood by the open window, looking up through the dark blue water and watching the fish as they splashed about with their fins and tails. She could see the moon and stars shining faintly, but through the water they looked larger than they do to our eyes.

When something like a black cloud passed between her and them, she knew that it was either a whale swimming over her head, or a ship full of human beings who never imagined that a pretty little mermaid was standing beneath them, holding out her white hands towards the keel of their ship.

At length the eldest was fifteen and was allowed to rise to the surface of the ocean.

When she returned she had hundreds of things to talk about. But the finest thing, she said, was to lie on a sand bank in the quiet moonlit sea, near the shore, gazing at the lights of the near-by town, that twinkled like hundreds of stars, and listening to the sounds of music, the noise of carriages, the voices of human beings, and the merry pealing of the bells in the church steeples. Because she could not go near all these wonderful things, she longed for them all the more.

Oh, how eagerly did the youngest sister listen to all these descriptions! And afterwards, when she stood at the open window looking up through the dark-blue water, she thought of the great city, with all its bustle and noise, and even fancied she could hear the sound of the church bells down in the depths of the sea.

In another year the second sister received permission to rise to the surface of the water and to swim about where she pleased. She rose just as the sun was setting, and this, she said, was the most beautiful sight of all. The whole sky looked like gold, and violet and rose-colored clouds, which she could not describe, drifted across it. And more swiftly than the clouds, flew a large flock of wild swans toward the setting sun, like a long white veil across the sea. She also swam towards the sun, but it sank into the waves, and the rosy tints faded from the clouds and from the sea.

The third sister's turn followed, and she was the boldest of them all, for she swam up a broad river that emptied into the sea. On the banks she saw green hills covered with beautiful vines, and palaces and castles peeping out from amid the proud trees of the forest. She heard birds singing and felt the rays of the sun so strongly that she was obliged often to dive under the water to cool her burning face.

In a narrow creek she found a large group of little human children, almost naked, sporting about in the water. She wanted to play with them, but they fled in a great fright; and then a little black animal—it was a dog, but she did not know it, for she had never seen one before—came to the water and barked at her so furiously that she became frightened and rushed back to the open sea. But she said she should never forget the beautiful forest, the green hills, and the pretty children who could swim in the water although they had no tails.

The fourth sister was more timid. She remained in the midst of the sea, but said it was quite as beautiful there as nearer the land. She could see many miles around her, and the sky above looked like a bell of glass. She had seen the ships, but at such a great distance that they looked like sea gulls. The dolphins sported in the waves, and the great whales spouted water from their nostrils till it seemed as if a hundred fountains were playing in every direction.

The fifth sister's birthday occurred in the winter, so when her turn came she saw what the others had not seen the first time they went up. The sea looked quite green, and large icebergs were floating about, each like a pearl, she said, but larger and loftier than the churches built by men. They were of the most singular shapes and glittered like diamonds. She had seated herself on one of the largest and let the wind play with her long hair.

She noticed that all the ships sailed past very rapidly, steering as far away as they could, as if they were afraid of the iceberg. Towards evening, as the sun went down, dark clouds covered the sky, the thunder rolled, and the flashes of lightning glowed red on the icebergs as they were tossed about by the heaving sea. On all the ships the sails were reefed with fear and trembling, while she sat on the floating iceberg, calmly watching the lightning as it darted its forked flashes into the sea.

Each of the sisters, when first she had permission to rise to the surface, was delighted with the new and beautiful sights. Now that they were grown-up girls and could go when they pleased, they had become quite indifferent about it. They soon wished themselves back again, and after a month had passed they said it was much more beautiful down below and pleasanter to be at home.

Yet often, in the evening hours, the five sisters would twine their arms about each other and rise to the surface together. Their voices were more charming than that of any human being, and before the approach of a storm, when they feared that a ship might be lost, they swam before the vessel, singing enchanting songs of the delights to be found in the depths of the sea and begging the voyagers not to fear if they sank to the bottom.

But the sailors could not understand the song and thought it was the sighing of the storm. These things were never beautiful to them, for if the ship sank, the men were drowned and their dead bodies alone reached the palace of the Sea King.

When the sisters rose, arm in arm, through the water, their youngest sister would stand quite alone, looking after them, ready to cry—only, since mermaids have no tears, she suffered more acutely.

"Oh, were I but fifteen years old!" said she. "I know that I shall love the world up there, and all the people who live in it."

At last she reached her fifteenth year.

"Well, now you are grown up," said the old dowager, her grandmother. "Come, and let me adorn you like your sisters." And she placed in her hair a wreath of white lilies, of which every flower leaf was half a pearl. Then the old lady ordered eight great oysters to attach themselves to the tail of the princess to show her high rank.

"But they hurt me so," said the little mermaid.

"Yes, I know; pride must suffer pain," replied the old lady.

Oh, how gladly she would have shaken off all this grandeur and laid aside the heavy wreath! The red flowers in her own garden would have suited her much better. But she could not change herself, so she said farewell and rose as lightly as a bubble to the surface of the water.

The sun had just set when she raised her head above the waves. The clouds were tinted with crimson and gold, and through the glimmering twilight beamed the evening star in all its beauty. The sea was calm, and the air mild and fresh. A large ship with three masts lay becalmed on the water; only one sail was set, for not a breeze stirred, and the sailors sat idle on deck or amidst the rigging. There was music and song on board, and as darkness came on, a hundred colored lanterns were lighted, as if the flags of all nations waved in the air.

The little mermaid swam close to the cabin windows, and now and then, as the waves lifted her up, she could look in through glass window-panes and see a number of gayly dressed people.

Among them, and the most beautiful of all, was a young prince with large, black eyes. He was sixteen years of age, and his birthday was being celebrated with great display. The sailors were dancing on deck, and when the prince came out of the cabin, more than a hundred rockets rose in the air, making it as bright as day. The little mermaid was so startled that she dived under water, and when she again stretched out her head, it looked as if all the stars of heaven were falling around her.

She had never seen such fireworks before. Great suns spurted fire about, splendid fireflies flew into the blue air, and everything was reflected in the clear, calm sea beneath. The ship itself was so brightly illuminated that all the people, and even the smallest rope, could be distinctly seen. How handsome the young prince looked, as he pressed the hands of all his guests and smiled at them, while the music resounded through the clear night air!

It was very late, yet the little mermaid could not take her eyes from the ship or from the beautiful prince. The colored lanterns had been extinguished, no more rockets rose in the air, and the cannon had ceased firing; but the sea became restless, and a moaning, grumbling sound could be heard beneath the waves. Still the little mermaid remained by the cabin window, rocking up and down on the water, so that she could look within. After a while the sails were quickly set, and the ship went on her way. But soon the waves rose higher, heavy clouds darkened the sky, and lightning appeared in the distance. A dreadful storm was approaching.

Once more the sails were furled, and the great ship pursued her flying course over the raging sea. The waves rose mountain high, as if they would overtop the mast, but the ship dived like a swan between them, then rose again on their lofty, foaming crests. To the little mermaid this was pleasant sport; but not so to the sailors. At length the ship groaned and creaked; the thick planks gave way under the lashing of the sea, as the waves broke over the deck; the mainmast snapped asunder like a reed, and as the ship lay over on her side, the water rushed in.

The little mermaid now perceived that the crew were in danger; even she was obliged to be careful, to avoid the beams and planks of the wreck which lay scattered on the water. At one moment it was pitch dark so that she could not see a single object, but when a flash of lightning came it revealed the whole scene; she could see every one who had been on board except the prince. When the ship parted, she had seen him sink into the deep waves, and she was glad, for she thought he would now be with her. Then she remembered that human beings could not live in the water, so that when he got down to her father's palace he would certainly be quite dead.

No, he must not die! So she swam about among the beams and planks which strewed the surface of the sea, forgetting that they could crush her to pieces. Diving deep under the dark waters, rising and falling with the waves, she at length managed to reach the young prince, who was fast losing the power to swim in that stormy sea. His limbs were failing him, his beautiful eyes were closed, and he would have died had not the little mermaid come to his assistance. She held his head above the water and let the waves carry them where they would.

In the morning the storm had ceased, but of the ship not a single fragment could be seen. The sun came up red and shining out of the water, and its beams brought back the hue of health to the prince's cheeks, but his eyes remained closed. The mermaid kissed his high, smooth forehead and stroked back his wet hair. He seemed to her like the marble statue in her little garden, so she kissed him again and wished that he might live.

Presently they came in sight of land, and she saw lofty blue mountains on which the white snow rested as if a flock of swans were lying upon them. Beautiful green forests were near the shore, and close by stood a large building, whether a church or a convent she could not tell. Orange and citron trees grew in the garden, and before the door stood lofty palms. The sea here formed a little bay, in which the water lay quiet and still, but very deep.

She swam with the handsome prince to the beach, which was covered with fine white sand, and there she laid him in the warm sunshine, taking care to raise his head higher than his body. Then bells sounded in the large white building, and some young girls came into the garden. The little mermaid swam out farther from the shore and hid herself among some high rocks that rose out of the water. Covering her head and neck with the foam of the sea, she watched there to see what would become of the poor prince.

It was not long before she saw a young girl approach the spot where the prince lay. She seemed frightened at first, but only for a moment; then she brought a number of people, and the mermaid saw that the prince came to life again and smiled upon those who stood about him. But to her he sent no smile; he knew not that she had saved him. This made her very sorrowful, and when he was led away into the great building, she dived down into the water and returned to her father's castle.

She had always been silent and thoughtful, and now she was more so than ever. Her sisters asked her what she had seen during her first visit to the surface of the water, but she could tell them nothing. Many an evening and morning did she rise to the place where she had left the prince. She saw the fruits in the garden ripen and watched them gathered; she watched the snow on the mountain tops melt away; but never did she see the prince, and therefore she always returned home more sorrowful than before.

It was her only comfort to sit in her own little garden and fling her arm around the beautiful marble statue, which was like the prince. She gave up tending her flowers, and they grew in wild confusion over the paths, twining their long leaves and stems round the branches of the trees so that the whole place became dark and gloomy.

At length she could bear it no longer and told one of her sisters all about it. Then the others heard the secret, and very soon it became known to several mermaids, one of whom had an intimate friend who happened to know about the prince. She had also seen the festival on board ship, and she told them where the prince came from and where his palace stood.

"Come, little sister," said the other princesses. Then they entwined their arms and rose together to the surface of the water, near the spot where they knew the prince's palace stood. It was built of bright-yellow, shining stone and had long flights of marble steps, one of which reached quite down to the sea.

Splendid gilded cupolas rose over the roof, and between the pillars that surrounded the whole building stood lifelike statues of marble. Through the clear crystal of the lofty windows could be seen noble rooms, with costly silk curtains and hangings of tapestry and walls covered with beautiful paintings. In the center of the largest salon a fountain threw its sparkling jets high up into the glass cupola of the ceiling, through which the sun shone in upon the water and upon the beautiful plants that grew in the basin of the fountain.

Now that the little mermaid knew where the prince lived, she spent many an evening and many a night on the water near the palace. She would swim much nearer the shore than any of the others had ventured, and once she went up the narrow channel under the marble balcony, which threw a broad shadow on the water. Here she sat and watched the young prince, who thought himself alone in the bright moonlight.

She often saw him evenings, sailing in a beautiful boat on which music sounded and flags waved. She peeped out from among the green rushes, and if the wind caught her long silvery-white veil, those who saw it believed it to be a swan, spreading out its wings.

Many a night, too, when the fishermen set their nets by the light of their torches, she heard them relate many good things about the young prince. And this made her glad that she had saved his life when he was tossed about half dead on the waves. She remembered how his head had rested on her bosom and how heartily she had kissed him, but he knew nothing of all this and could not even dream of her.

She grew more and more to like human beings and wished more and more to be able to wander about with those whose world seemed to be so much larger than her own. They could fly over the sea in ships and mount the high hills which were far above the clouds; and the lands they possessed, their woods and their fields, stretched far away beyond the reach of her sight. There was so much that she wished to know! but her sisters were unable to answer all her questions. She then went to her old grandmother, who knew all about the upper world, which she rightly called "the lands above the sea."

"If human beings are not drowned," asked the little mermaid, "can they live forever? Do they never die, as we do here in the sea?"

"Yes," replied the old lady, "they must also die, and their term of life is even shorter than ours. We sometimes live for three hundred years, but when we cease to exist here, we become only foam on the surface of the water and have not even a grave among those we love. We have not immortal souls, we shall never live again; like the green seaweed when once it has been cut off, we can never flourish more. Human beings, on the contrary, have souls which live forever, even after the body has been turned to dust. They rise up through the clear, pure air, beyond the glittering stars. As we rise out of the water and behold all the land of the earth, so do they rise to unknown and glorious regions which we shall never see."

"Why have not we immortal souls?" asked the little mermaid, mournfully. "I would gladly give all the hundreds of years that I have to live, to be a human being only for one day and to have the hope of knowing the happiness of that glorious world above the stars."

"You must not think that," said the old woman. "We believe that we are much happier and much better off than human beings."

"So I shall die," said the little mermaid, "and as the foam of the sea I shall be driven about, never again to hear the music of the waves or to see the pretty flowers or the red sun? Is there anything I can do to win an immortal soul?"

"No," said the old woman; "unless a man should love you so much that you were more to him than his father or his mother, and if all his thoughts and all his love were fixed upon you, and the priest placed his right hand in yours, and he promised to be true to you here and hereafter—then his soul would glide into your body, and you would obtain a share in the future happiness of mankind. He would give to you a soul and retain his own as well; but this can never happen. Your fish's tail, which among us is considered so beautiful, on earth is thought to be quite ugly. They do not know any better, and they think it necessary, in order to be handsome, to have two stout props, which they call legs."

Then the little mermaid sighed and looked sorrowfully at her fish's tail. "Let us be happy," said the old lady, "and dart and spring about during the three hundred years that we have to live, which is really quite long enough. After that we can rest ourselves all the better. This evening we are going to have a court ball."

It was one of those splendid sights which we can never see on earth. The walls and the ceiling of the large ballroom were of thick but transparent crystal. Many hundreds of colossal shells,—some of a deep red, others of a grass green,—with blue fire in them, stood in rows on each side. These lighted up the whole salon, and shone through the walls so that the sea was also illuminated. Innumerable fishes, great and small, swam past the crystal walls; on some of them the scales glowed with a purple brilliance, and on others shone like silver and gold. Through the halls flowed a broad stream, and in it danced the mermen and the mermaids to the music of their own sweet singing.

No one on earth has such lovely voices as they, but the little mermaid sang more sweetly than all. The whole court applauded her with hands and tails, and for a moment her heart felt quite gay, for she knew she had the sweetest voice either on earth or in the sea. But soon she thought again of the world above her; she could not forget the charming prince, nor her sorrow that she had not an immortal soul like his.

She crept away silently out of her father's palace, and while everything within was gladness and song, she sat in her own little garden, sorrowful and alone. Then she heard the bugle sounding through the water and thought: "He is certainly sailing above, he in whom my wishes center and in whose hands I should like to place the happiness of my life. I will venture all for him and to win an immortal soul. While my sisters are dancing in my father's palace I will go to the sea witch, of whom I have always been so much afraid; she can give me counsel and help."

Then the little mermaid went out from her garden and took the road to the foaming whirlpools, behind which the sorceress lived. She had never been that way before. Neither flowers nor grass grew there; nothing but bare, gray, sandy ground stretched out to the whirlpool, where the water, like foaming mill wheels, seized everything that came within its reach and cast it into the fathomless deep. Through the midst of these crushing whirlpools the little mermaid was obliged to pass before she could reach the dominions of the sea witch. Then, for a long distance, the road lay across a stretch of warm, bubbling mire, called by the witch her turf moor.

Beyond this was the witch's house, which stood in the center of a strange forest, where all the trees and flowers were polypi, half animals and half plants. They looked like serpents with a hundred heads, growing out of the ground. The branches were long, slimy arms, with fingers like flexible worms, moving limb after limb from the root to the top. All that could be reached in the sea they seized upon and held fast, so that it never escaped from their clutches.

The little mermaid was so alarmed at what she saw that she stood still and her heart beat with fear. She came very near turning back, but she thought of the prince and of the human soul for which she longed, and her courage returned. She fastened her long, flowing hair round her head, so that the polypi should not lay hold of it. She crossed her hands on her bosom, and then darted forward as a fish shoots through the water, between the supple arms and fingers of the ugly polypi, which were stretched out on each side of her.

She saw that they all held in their grasp something they had seized with their numerous little arms, which were as strong as iron bands. Tightly grasped in their clinging arms were white skeletons of human beings who had perished at sea and had sunk down into the deep waters; skeletons of land animals; and oars, rudders, and chests, of ships. There was even a little mermaid whom they had caught and strangled, and this seemed the most shocking of all to the little princess.

She now came to a space of marshy ground in the wood, where large, fat water snakes were rolling in the mire and showing their ugly, drab-colored bodies. In the midst of this spot stood a house, built of the bones of shipwrecked human beings. There sat the sea witch, allowing a toad to eat from her mouth just as people sometimes feed a canary with pieces of sugar. She called the ugly water snakes her little chickens and allowed them to crawl all over her bosom.

"I know what you want," said the sea witch. "It is very stupid of you, but you shall have your way, though it will bring you to sorrow, my pretty princess. You want to get rid of your fish's tail and to have two supports instead, like human beings on earth, so that the young prince may fall in love with you and so that you may have an immortal soul." And then the witch laughed so loud and so disgustingly that the toad and the snakes fell to the ground and lay there wriggling.

"You are but just in time," said the witch, "for after sunrise to-morrow I should not be able to help you till the end of another year. I will prepare a draft for you, with which you must swim to land to-morrow before sunrise; seat yourself there and drink it. Your tail will then disappear, and shrink up into what men call legs.

"You will feel great pain, as if a sword were passing through you. But all who see you will say that you are the prettiest little human being they ever saw. You will still have the same floating gracefulness of movement, and no dancer will ever tread so lightly. Every step you take, however, will be as if you were treading upon sharp knives and as if the blood must flow. If you will bear all this, I will help you."

"Yes, I will," said the little princess in a trembling voice, as she thought of the prince and the immortal soul.

"But think again," said the witch, "for when once your shape has become like a human being, you can no more be a mermaid. You will never return through the water to your sisters or to your father's palace again. And if you do not win the love of the prince, so that he is willing to forget his father and mother for your sake and to love you with his whole soul and allow the priest to join your hands that you may be man and wife, then you will never have an immortal soul. The first morning after he marries another, your heart will break and you will become foam on the crest of the waves."

"I will do it," said the little mermaid, and she became pale as death.

"But I must be paid, also," said the witch, "and it is not a trifle that I ask. You have the sweetest voice of any who dwell here in the depths of the sea, and you believe that you will be able to charm the prince with it. But this voice you must give to me. The best thing you possess will I have as the price of my costly draft, which must be mixed with my own blood so that it may be as sharp as a two-edged sword."

"But if you take away my voice," said the little mermaid, "what is left for me?"

"Your beautiful form, your graceful walk, and your expressive eyes. Surely with these you can enchain a man's heart.

69

Well, have you lost your courage? Put out your little tongue, that I may cut it off as my payment; then you shall have the powerful draft."

"It shall be," said the little mermaid.

Then the witch placed her caldron on the fire, to prepare the magic draft.

"Cleanliness is a good thing," said she, scouring the vessel with snakes which she had tied together in a large knot. Then she pricked herself in the breast and let the black blood drop into the caldron. The steam that rose twisted itself into such horrible shapes that no one could look at them without fear. Every moment the witch threw a new ingredient into the vessel, and when it began to boil, the sound was like the weeping of a crocodile. When at last the magic draft was ready, it looked like the clearest water.

"There it is for you," said the witch. Then she cut off the mermaid's tongue, so that she would never again speak or sing. "If the polypi should seize you as you return through the wood," said the witch, "throw over them a few drops of the potion, and their fingers will be torn into a thousand pieces." But the little mermaid had no occasion to do this, for the polypi sprang back in terror when they caught sight of the glittering draft, which shone in her hand like a twinkling star.

So she passed quickly through the wood and the marsh and between the rushing whirlpools. She saw that in her father's palace the torches in the ballroom were extinguished and that all within were asleep. But she did not venture to go in to them, for now that she was dumb and going to leave them forever she felt as if her heart would break. She stole into the garden, took a flower from the flower bed of each of her sisters, kissed her hand towards the palace a thousand times, and then rose up through the dark-blue waters.

The sun had not risen when she came in sight of the prince's palace and approached the beautiful marble steps, but the moon shone clear and bright. Then the little mermaid drank the magic draft, and it seemed as if a two-edged sword went through her delicate body. She fell into a swoon and lay like one dead. When the sun rose and shone over the sea, she recovered and felt a sharp pain, but before her stood the handsome young prince.

He fixed his coal-black eyes upon her so earnestly that she cast down her own and then became aware that her fish's tail was gone and that she had as pretty a pair of white legs and tiny feet as any little maiden could have. But she had no clothes, so she wrapped herself in her long, thick hair. The prince asked her who she was and whence she came. She looked at him mildly and sorrowfully with her deep blue eyes, but could not speak. He took her by the hand and led her to the palace.

Every step she took was as the witch had said it would be; she felt as if she were treading upon the points of needles or sharp knives. She bore it willingly, however, and moved at the prince's side as lightly as a bubble, so that he and all who saw her wondered at her graceful, swaying movements. She was very soon arrayed in costly robes of silk and muslin and was the most beautiful creature in the palace; but she was dumb and could neither speak nor sing.

Beautiful female slaves, dressed in silk and gold, stepped forward and sang before the prince and his royal parents. One sang better than all the others, and the prince clapped his hands and smiled at her. This was a great sorrow to the little mermaid, for she knew how much more sweetly she herself once could sing, and she thought, "Oh, if he could only know that I have given away my voice forever, to be with him!"

The slaves next performed some pretty fairy-like dances, to the sound of beautiful music. Then the little mermaid raised her lovely white arms, stood on the tips of her toes, glided over the floor, and danced as no one yet had been able to dance. At each moment her beauty was more revealed, and her expressive eyes appealed more directly to the heart than the songs of the slaves. Every one was enchanted, especially the prince, who called her his little foundling. She danced again quite readily, to please him, though each time her foot touched the floor it seemed as if she trod on sharp knives.

The prince said she should remain with him always, and she was given permission to sleep at his door, on a velvet cushion. He had a page's dress made for her, that she might accompany him on horseback. They rode together through the sweet-scented woods, where the green boughs touched their shoulders, and the little birds sang among the fresh leaves.

She climbed with him to the tops of high mountains, and although her tender feet bled so that even her steps were marked, she only smiled, and followed him till they could see the clouds beneath them like a flock of birds flying to distant lands. While at the prince's palace, and when all the household were asleep, she would go and sit on the broad marble steps, for it eased her burning feet to bathe them in the cold sea water. It was then that she thought of all those below in the deep.

Once during the night her sisters came up arm in arm, singing sorrowfully as they floated on the water. She beckoned to them, and they recognized her and told her how she had grieved them; after that, they came to the same place every night. Once she saw in the distance her old grandmother, who had not been to the surface of the sea for many years, and the old Sea King, her father, with his crown on his head. They stretched out their hands towards her, but did not venture so near the land as her sisters had.

As the days passed she loved the prince more dearly, and he loved her as one would love a little child. The thought never came to him to make her his wife. Yet unless he married her, she could not receive an immortal soul, and on the morning after his marriage with another, she would dissolve into the foam of the sea.

"Do you not love me the best of them all?" the eyes of the little mermaid seemed to say when he took her in his arms and kissed her fair forehead.

"Yes, you are dear to me," said the prince, "for you have the best heart and you are the most devoted to me. You are like a young maiden whom I once saw, but whom I shall never meet again. I was in a ship that was wrecked, and the waves cast me ashore near a holy temple where several young maidens performed the service. The youngest of them found me on the shore and saved my life. I saw her but twice, and she is the only one in the world whom I could love. But you are like her, and you have almost driven her image from my mind. She belongs to the holy temple, and good fortune has sent you to me in her stead. We will never part.

"Ah, he knows not that it was I who saved his life," thought the little mermaid. "I carried him over the sea to the wood where the temple stands; I sat beneath the foam and watched till the human beings came to help him. I saw the pretty maiden that he loves better than he loves me." The mermaid sighed deeply, but she could not weep. "He says the maiden belongs to the holy temple, therefore she will never return to the world—they will meet no more. I am by his side and see him every day. I will take care of him, and love him, and give up my life for his sake."

Very soon it was said that the prince was to marry and that the beautiful daughter of a neighboring king would be his wife, for a fine ship was being fitted out. Although the prince gave out that he intended merely to pay a visit to the king, it was generally supposed that he went to court the princess. A great company were to go with him. The little mermaid smiled and shook her head. She knew the prince's thoughts better than any of the others.

"I must travel," he had said to her; "I must see this beautiful princess. My parents desire it, but they will not oblige me to bring her home as my bride. I cannot love her, because she is not like the beautiful maiden in the temple, whom you resemble. If I were forced to choose a bride, I would choose you, my dumb foundling, with those expressive eyes." Then he kissed her rosy mouth, played with her long, waving hair, and laid his head on her heart, while she dreamed of human happiness and an immortal soul.

"You are not afraid of the sea, my dumb child, are you?" he said, as they stood on the deck of the noble ship which was to carry them to the country of the neighboring king. Then he told her of storm and of calm, of strange fishes in the deep beneath them, and of what the divers had seen there. She smiled at his descriptions, for she knew better than any one what wonders were at the bottom of the sea.

In the moonlight night, when all on board were asleep except the man at the helm, she sat on deck, gazing down through the clear water. She thought she could distinguish her father's castle, and upon it her aged grandmother, with the silver crown on her head, looking through the rushing tide at the keel of the vessel. Then her sisters came up on the waves and gazed at her mournfully, wringing their white hands. She beckoned to them, and smiled, and wanted to tell them how happy and well off she was. But the cabin boy approached, and when her sisters dived down, he thought what he saw was only the foam of the sea.

The next morning the ship sailed into the harbor of a beautiful town belonging to the king whom the prince was going to visit. The church bells were ringing, and from the high towers sounded a flourish of trumpets. Soldiers, with flying colors and glittering bayonets, lined the roads through which they passed. Every day was a festival, balls and entertainments following one another. But the princess had not yet appeared. People said that she had been brought up and educated in a religious house, where she was learning every royal virtue.

At last she came. Then the little mermaid, who was anxious to see whether she was really beautiful, was obliged to admit that she had never seen a more perfect vision of beauty. Her skin was delicately fair, and beneath her long, dark eyelashes her laughing blue eyes shone with truth and purity.

"It was you," said the prince, "who saved my life when I lay as if dead on the beach," and he folded his blushing bride in his arms.

"Oh, I am too happy!" said he to the little mermaid; "my fondest hopes are now fulfilled. You will rejoice at my happiness, for your devotion to me is great and sincere."

The little mermaid kissed his hand and felt as if her heart were already broken. His wedding morning would bring death to her, and she would change into the foam of the sea.

All the church bells rang, and the heralds rode through the town proclaiming the betrothal.

Perfumed oil was burned in costly silver lamps on every altar. The priests waved the censers, while the bride and the bridegroom joined their hands and received the blessing of the bishop. The little mermaid, dressed in silk and gold, held up the bride's train; but her ears heard nothing of the festive music, and her eyes saw not the holy ceremony. She thought of the night of death which was coming to her, and of all she had lost in the world.

On the same evening the bride and bridegroom went on board the ship. Cannons were roaring, flags waving, and in the center of the ship a costly tent of purple and gold had been erected. It contained elegant sleeping couches for the bridal pair during the night. The ship, under a favorable wind, with swelling sails, glided away smoothly and lightly over the calm sea.

When it grew dark, a number of colored lamps were lighted and the sailors danced merrily on the deck. The little mermaid could not help thinking of her first rising out of the sea, when she had seen similar joyful festivities, so she too joined in the dance, poised herself in the air as a swallow when he pursues his prey, and all present cheered her wonderingly. She had never danced so gracefully before. Her tender feet felt as if cut with sharp knives, but she cared not for the pain; a sharper pang had pierced her heart.

She knew this was the last evening she should ever see the prince for whom she had forsaken her kindred and her home. She had given up her beautiful voice and suffered unheard-of pain daily for him, while he knew nothing of it. This was the last evening that she should breathe the same air with him or gaze on the starry sky and the deep sea. An eternal night, without a thought or a dream, awaited her. She had no soul, and now could never win one.

All was joy and gaiety on the ship until long after midnight. She smiled and danced with the rest, while the thought of death was in her heart. The prince kissed his beautiful bride and she played with his raven hair till they went arm in arm to rest in the sumptuous tent. Then all became still on board the ship, and only the pilot, who stood at the helm, was awake.

The little mermaid leaned her white arms on the edge of the vessel and looked towards the east for the first blush of morning—for that first ray of the dawn which was to be her death. She saw her sisters rising out of the flood. They were as pale as she, but their beautiful hair no longer waved in the wind; it had been cut off.

"We have given our hair to the witch," said they, "to obtain help for you, that you may not die to-night. She has given us a knife; see, it is very sharp. Before the sun rises you must plunge it into the heart of the prince. When the warm blood falls upon your feet they will grow together again into a fish's tail, and you will once more be a mermaid and can return to us to live out your three hundred years before you are changed into the salt sea foam. Haste, then; either he or you must die before sunrise. Our old grandmother mourns so for you that her white hair is falling, as ours fell under the witch's scissors. Kill the prince, and come back. Hasten! Do you not see the first red streaks in the sky? In a few minutes the sun will rise, and you must die."

Then they sighed deeply and mournfully, and sank beneath the waves.

The little mermaid drew back the crimson curtain of the tent and beheld the fair bride, whose head was resting on the prince's breast. She bent down and kissed his noble brow, then looked at the sky, on which the rosy dawn grew brighter and brighter. She glanced at the sharp knife and again fixed her eyes on the prince, who whispered the name of his bride in his dreams.

She was in his thoughts, and the knife trembled in the hand of the little mermaid—but she flung it far from her into the waves. The water turned red where it fell, and the drops that spurted up looked like blood. She cast one more lingering, half-fainting glance at the prince, then threw herself from the ship into the sea and felt her body dissolving into foam.

The sun rose above the waves, and his warm rays fell on the cold foam of the little mermaid, who did not feel as if she were dying. She saw the bright sun, and hundreds of transparent, beautiful creatures floating around her—she could see through them the white sails of the ships and the red clouds in the sky. Their speech was melodious, but could not be heard by mortal ears—just as their bodies could not be seen by mortal eyes. The little mermaid perceived that she had a body like theirs and that she continued to rise higher and higher out of the foam. "Where am I?" asked she, and her voice sounded ethereal, like the voices of those who were with her. No earthly music could imitate it.

"Among the daughters of the air," answered one of them. "A mermaid has not an immortal soul, nor can she obtain one unless she wins the love of a human being. On the will of another hangs her eternal destiny. But the daughters of the air, although they do not possess an immortal soul, can, by their good deeds, procure one for themselves. We fly to warm countries and cool the sultry air that destroys mankind with the pestilence. We carry the perfume of the flowers to spread health and restoration.

"After we have striven for three hundred years to do all the good in our power, we receive an immortal soul and take part in the happiness of mankind. You, poor little mermaid, have tried with your whole heart to do as we are doing.

You have suffered and endured, and raised yourself to the spirit world by your good deeds, and now, by striving for three hundred years in the same way, you may obtain an immortal soul."

The little mermaid lifted her glorified eyes toward the sun and, for the first time, felt them filling with tears.

On the ship in which she had left the prince there were life and noise, and she saw him and his beautiful bride searching for her. Sorrowfully they gazed at the pearly foam, as if they knew she had thrown herself into the waves. Unseen she kissed the forehead of the bride and fanned the prince, and then mounted with the other children of the air to a rosy cloud that floated above.

"After three hundred years, thus shall we float into the kingdom of heaven," said she. "And we may even get there sooner," whispered one of her companions. "Unseen we can enter the houses of men where there are children, and for every day on which we find a good child that is the joy of his parents and deserves their love, our time of probation is shortened. The child does not know, when we fly through the room, that we smile with joy at his good conduct—for we can count one year less of our three hundred years. But when we see a naughty or a wicked child we shed tears of sorrow, and for every tear a day is added to our time of trial."

The Ice-Maiden

Let us visit Switzerland and look around us in the glorious country of mountains, where the forest rises out of steep rocky walls; let us ascend to the dazzling snow-fields, and thence descend to the green plains, where the rivulets and brooks hasten away, foaming up, as if they feared not to vanish, as they reached the sea.

The sun beams upon the deep valley, it burns also upon the heavy masses of snow; so that after the lapse of years, they melt into shining ice-blocks, and become rolling avalanches and heaped-up glaciers.

Two of these lie in the broad clefts of the rock, under the Schreckhorn and Wetterhorn, near the little town of Grindelwald. They are so remarkable that many strangers come to gaze at them, in the summer time, from all parts of the world; they come over the high snow-covered mountains, they come from the deepest valleys, and they are obliged to ascend during many hours, and as they ascend, the valley sinks deeper and deeper, as though seen from an air-balloon.

Far around the peaks of the mountains, the clouds often hang like heavy curtains of smoke; whilst down in the valley, where the many brown wooden houses lie scattered about, a sun-beam shines, and here and there brings out a tiny spot, in radiant green, as though it were transparent. The water roars, froths and foams below, the water hums and tinkles above, and it looks as if silver ribbons were fluttering over the cliffs.

On each side of the way, as one ascends, are wooden houses; each house has a little potato-garden, and that is a necessity, for in the door-way are many little mouths. There are plenty of children, and they can consume abundance of food; they rush out of the houses, and throng about the travelers, come they on foot or in carriage. The whole horde of children traffic; the little ones offer prettily carved wooden houses, for sale, similar to those they build on the mountains. Rain or shine, the children assemble with their wares.

Some twenty years ago, there stood here, several times, a little boy, who wished to sell his toys, but he always kept aloof from the other children; he stood with serious countenance and with both hands tightly clasped around his wooden box, as if he feared it would slip away from him; but on account of this gravity, and because the boy was so small, it caused him to be remarked, and often he made the best bargain, without knowing why. His grandfather lived still higher in the mountains, and it was he who carved the pretty wooden houses.

There stood in the room, an old cup-board, full of carvings; there were nut-crackers, knives, spoons, and boxes with delicate foliage, and leaping chamois; there was everything, which could rejoice a merry child's eye, but this little fellow, (he was named Rudy) looked at and desired only the old gun under the rafters. His grandfather had said, that he should have it some day, but that he must first grow big and strong enough to use it.

Small as the boy was, he was obliged to take care of the goats, and if he who can climb with them is a good guardian, well then indeed was Rudy. Why he climbed even higher than they! He loved to take the bird's nests from the trees, high in the air, for he was bold and daring; and he only smiled when he stood by the roaring water-fall, or when he heard a rolling avalanche.

He never played with the other children; he only met them, when his grandfather sent him out to sell his carvings, and Rudy took but little interest in this; he much preferred to wander about the rocks, or to sit and listen to his grandfather relate about old times and about the inhabitants of Meiringen, where he came from. He said that these people had not been there since the beginning of the world; they had come from the far North, where the race called Swedes, dwelt.

To know this, was indeed great wisdom, and Rudy knew this; but he became still wiser, through the intercourse which he had with the other occupants of the house—belonging to the animal race. There was a large dog, Ajola, an heir-loom from Rudy's father; and a cat, and she was of great importance to Rudy, for she had taught him to climb.

"Come out on the roof!" said the cat, quite plain and distinctly, for when one is a child, and can not yet speak, one understands the hens and ducks, the cats and dogs remarkably well; they speak for us as intelligibly as father or mother. One needs but to be little, and then even grandfather's stick can neigh, and become a horse, with head, legs and tail. With some children, this knowledge slips away later than with others, and people say of these, that they are very backward, that they remain children fearfully long.—People say so many things!

"Come with me, little Rudy, out on the roof!" was about the first thing that the cat said, that Rudy understood. "It is all imagination about falling; one does not fall, when one does not fear to do so. Come, place your one paw so, and your other so! Take care of your fore-paws! Look sharp with your eyes, and give suppleness to your limbs! If there be a hole, jump, hold fast, that's the way I do!"

And Rudy did so, and that was the reason that he sat out on the roof with the cat so often; he sat with her in the tree-tops, yes, he sat on the edge of the rocks, where the cats could not come. "Higher, higher!" said the trees and bushes. "See, how we climb! how high we go, how firm we hold on, even on the outermost peaks of the rocks!"

And Rudy went generally on the mountain before the sun rose, and then he got his morning drink, the fresh, strengthening mountain air, the drink, that our Lord only can prepare, and men can read its recipe, and thus it stands written: "the fresh scent of the herbs of the mountains and the mint and thyme of the valleys."

All heaviness is imbibed by the hanging clouds, and the wind sends it out like grape-shot into the fir-woods; the fragrant breeze becomes perfume, light and fresh and ever fresher—that was Rudy's morning drink.

The blessing bringing daughters of the Sun, the sun-beams, kissed his cheeks, and Vertigo stood and watched, but dared not approach him; and the swallows below from grandfather's house, where there were no less than seven nests, flew up to him and the goats, and they sang: "We and you! and you and we!" They brought greetings from home, even from the two hens, the only birds in the room; with whom however Rudy never had intercourse.

Little as he was, he had traveled, and not a little, for so small a boy; he was born in the Canton Valais, and had been carried from there over the mountains. Lately he had visited the Staubbach, which waves in the air like a silver gauze, before the snow decked, dazzling white mountain: "the Jungfrau." And he had been in Grindelwald, near the great glaciers; but that was a sad story. There, his mother had found her death, and, "little Rudy," so said his grandfather, "had lost his childish merriment." "When the boy was not a year old, he laughed more than he cried," so wrote his mother, "but since he was in the ice-gap, quite another mind has come over him." His grand-father did not like to speak on the subject, but every one on the mountain knew all about it.

Rudy's father had been a postilion, and the large dog in the room, had always followed him on his journeys to the lake of Geneva, over the Simplon. In the valley of the Rhone, in Canton Valais, still lived Rudy's family, on his father's side, and his father's brother was a famous chamois hunter and a well-known guide. Rudy was only a year old, when he lost his father, and his mother longed to return to her relations in Berner Oberlande. Her father lived a few hours walk from Grindelwald; he was a carver in wood, and earned enough by it to live. In the month of June, carrying her little child, she started homewards,

Accompanied by two chamois hunters; intending to cross the Gemmi on their way to Grindelwald. They already had accomplished the longer part of their journey, had passed the high ridges, had come to the snow-plains, they already saw the valley of their home, with its well-known wooden houses, and had now but to reach the summit of one of the great glaciers. The snow had freshly fallen and concealed a cleft,—which did not lead to the deepest abyss, where the water roared—but still deeper than man could reach. The young woman, who was holding her child, slipped, sank and was gone; one heard no cry, no sigh, nought but a little child weeping.

More than an hour elapsed, before her companions could bring poles and ropes, from the nearest house, in order to afford assistance. After great exertion they drew from the ice-gap, what appeared to be two lifeless bodies; every means were employed and they succeeded in calling the child back to life, but not the mother. So the old grandfather received instead of a daughter, a daughter's son in his house; the little one, who laughed more than he wept, but, who now, seemed to have lost this custom. A change in him, had certainly taken place, in the cleft of the glacier, in the wonderful cold world; where, according to the belief of the Swiss peasant, the souls of the damned are incarcerated until the day of judgment.

Not unlike water, which after long journeying, has been compressed into blocks of green glass, the glaciers lie here, so that one huge mass of ice is heaped on the other. The rushing stream roars below and melts snow and ice; within, hollow caverns and mighty clefts open, this is a wonderful palace of ice, and in it dwells the Ice-Maiden, the Queen of the glaciers.

She, the murderess, the destroyer, is half a child of air and half the powerful ruler of the streams; therefore, she had received the power, to elevate herself with the speed of the chamois to the highest pinnacle of the snow-topped mountain; where the most daring mountaineer had to hew his way, in order to take firm foot-hold. She sails up the rushing river on a slender fir-branch—springs from one cliff to another, with her long snow-white hair, fluttering around her, and with her bluish-green mantle, which resembles the water of the deep Swiss lakes.

"Crush, hold fast! the power is mine!" cried she. "They have stolen a lovely boy from me, a boy, whom I had kissed, but not kissed to death. He is again with men, he tends the goats on the mountains; he climbs up, up high, beyond the reach of all others, but not beyond mine! He is mine, I shall have him!" —

And she ordered Vertigo to fulfill her duty; it was too warm for the Ice-Maiden, in summer-time, in the green spots where the mint thrives. Vertigo arose; one came, three came, (for Vertigo had many sisters, very many of them) and the Maiden chose the strongest among those that rule within doors and without. They sit on the balusters and on the spires of the steep towers, they tread through the air as the swimmer glides through the water and entice their prey down the abyss.

Vertigo and the Ice-Maiden seize on men as the polypus clutches at all within its reach. Vertigo was to gain possession of Rudy. "Yes, just catch him for me" said Vertigo. "I cannot do it! The cat, the dirty thing, has taught him her arts! The child of the race of man, possesses a power, that repulses me; I cannot get at the little boy, when he hangs by the branches over the abyss. I may tickle him on the soles of his feet or give him a box on the ear whilst he is swinging in the air, it is of no avail. I can do nothing!"

"We *can* do it!" said the Ice-Maiden. "You or I! I! I!" —

"No, no!" sounded back the echo of the church-bells through the mountain, like a sweet melody; it was like speech, an harmonious chorus of all the spirits of nature, mild, good, full of love, for it came from the daughters of the sun-beams, who encamped themselves every evening in a circle around the pinnacles of the mountains, and spread out their rose-colored wings, that grow more and more red as the sun sinks, and glow over the high Alps; men call it, "the Alpine glow." When the sun is down, they enter the peaks of the rocks and sleep on the white snow, until the sun rises, and then they sally forth. Above all, they love flowers, butterflies, and men, and amongst them they had chosen little Rudy as their favorite.

"You will not catch him! You shall not have him!" said they. "I have caught and kept stronger and larger ones!" said the Ice-Maiden.

Then the daughters of the Sun sang a lay of the wanderer, whose cloak the whirlwind had torn off and carried away. The wind took the covering, but not the man. "Ye children of strength can seize, but not hold him; he is stronger, he is more spirit-like, than we; he ascends higher than the Sun, our mother! He possesses the magic word, that restrains wind and water, so that they are obliged to obey and serve him!"

So sounded cheerfully the bell-like chorus.

And every morning the sun-beams shone through the tiny window in the grandfather's house, on the quiet child. The daughters of the sun-beams kissed him, they wished to thaw him, to warm him and to carry away with them the icy kiss, which the queenly maiden of the glaciers had given him, as he lay on his dead mother's lap, in the deep icy gap, whence he was saved through a miracle.

II. THE JOURNEY TO THE NEW HOME.

Rudy was now eight years old. His father's brother, in Rhonethal, the other side of the mountain, wished to have the boy, for he thought that with him he would fare and prosper better; his grandfather perceived this and gave his consent.

Rudy must go. There were others to take leave of him, besides his grandfather; first there was Ajola, the old dog.

"Your father was post-boy and I was post-dog," said Ajola. "We have travelled up and down; I know dogs and men on the other side of the mountain. It is not my custom to speak much, but now, that we shall not have much time to converse with each other, I must talk a little more than usual. I will relate a story to you; I shall tell you how I have earned my bread, and how I have eaten it. I do not understand it and I suppose that you will not either, but it matters not, for I have discovered that the good things of this earth are not equally divided between dogs or men.

All are not fitted to lie on the lap and sip milk, I have not been accustomed to it; but I saw a little dog seated in the coach with us and it occupied a person's place. The woman who was its mistress, or who belonged to its mistress, had a bottle filled with milk, out of which she fed it; it got sweet sugar biscuits too, but it would not even eat them; only snuffed at them, and so the woman ate them herself. I ran in the mud, by the side of the coach, as hungry as a dog could be; I chewed my crude thoughts, that was not right—but this is often done! If I could but have been carried on some one's knee and have been seated in a coach! But one cannot have all one desires. I have not been able to do so, neither with barking nor with yawning."

That was Ajola's speech, and Rudy seized him by the neck and kissed him on his moist mouth, and then he took the cat in his arms, but she was angry at it.

"You are getting too strong for me, and I will not use my claws against you! Just climb over the mountains, I taught you to climb! Never think that you will fall, then you are secure!"

Then the cat ran away, without letting Rudy see how her grief shone out of her eye.

The hens ran about the floor; one had lost her tail; a traveller, who wished to be a hunter, had shot it off, because the creature had taken the hen for a bird of prey!

"Rudy is going over the mountain!" said one hen. "He is always in a hurry," said the other, "and I do not care for leave-takings!" and so they both tripped away.

And the goats, too, said farewell and cried: "Mit, mit, mah!" and that was so sad.

There were two nimble guides in the neighborhood, and they were about to cross the mountains; they were to descend to the other side of the Gemmi, and Rudy followed them on foot. This was a severe march for such a little chap, but he had strength and courage, and felt not fatigue.

The swallows accompanied them a part of the way. They sang: "We and you!

You and us!" The road went over the rapid Lütschine, which rushes forth from the black clefts of the glacier of Grindelwald, in many little streams. The fallen timber and the quarry-stones serve as bridges; they pass the alder-bush and descend the mountain where the glacier has detached itself from the mountain side; they cross over the glacier, over the blocks of ice, and go around them.

Rudy was obliged to creep a little, to walk a little, his eyes sparkled with delight, and he trod as firmly with his iron-shod mountain shoes, as though he wished to leave his foot-prints where he had stepped. The black mud which the mountain stream had poured upon the glacier gave it a cal-cined appearance, but the bluish-green, glassy ice still shone through it. They were obliged to go around the little ponds which were dammed up by blocks of ice; during these wanderings they came too near a large stone, which lay tottering on the brink of a crevice in the ice. The stone lost its equilibrium, it fell, rolled and the echo resounded from the deep hollow paths of the glacier.

Up, ever up; the glacier stretched itself on high—as a river, of wildly heaped up masses of ice, compressed among the steep cliffs. For an instant Rudy thought on what they had told him, about his having laid with his mother, in one of these cold-breathing chasms. Such thoughts soon vanished; it seemed to him as though it were some other story—one of the many which had been related to him.

Now and then, when the men thought that the ascent was too difficult for the little lad, they would reach him their hand, but he was never weary and stood on the slippery ice as firm as a chamois. Now they reached the bottom of the rocks, they were soon among the bare stones, which were void of moss; soon under the low fir-trees and again out on the green common—ever changing, ever new. Around them arose the snow mountains, whose names were as familiar to Rudy as they were to every child in the neighborhood: "the Jungfrau," "the Mönch," and "the Eiger."

Rudy had never been so high before, had never before trodden on the vast sea of snow, which lay there with its immoveable waves. The wind blew single flakes about, as it blows the foam upon the waters of the sea.

Glacier stood by glacier, if one may say so, hand in hand; each one was an ice-palace for the Ice-Maiden, whose power and will is: "to catch and to bury." The sun burned warmly, the snow was dazzling, as if sown with bluish-white, glittering diamond sparks. Countless insects (butterflies and bees mostly) lay in masses dead on the snow; they had ventured too high, or the wind had borne them thither, but to breathe their last in these cold regions.

A threatening cloud hung over the Wetterhorn, like a fine, black tuft of wool. It lowered itself slowly, heavily, with that which lay concealed within it, and this was the "Föhn,"[A] powerful in its strength when it broke loose. The impression of the entire journey, the night quarters above and then the road beyond, the deep rocky chasms, where the water forced its way through the blocks of stone with terrible rapidity, engraved itself indelibly on Rudy's mind.

On the other side of the sea of snow, a forsaken stone hut gave them protection and shelter for the night; a fire was quickly lighted, for they found within it charcoal and fir branches; they arranged their couch as well as possible. The men seated themselves around the fire, smoked their tobacco and drank the warm spicy drink, which they had prepared for themselves.

Rudy had his share too and they told him of the mysterious beings of the Alpine country; of the singular fighting snakes in the deep lakes; of the people of night; of the hordes of specters, who carry sleepers through the air, towards the wonderful floating city of Venice; of the wild shepherd, who drives his black sheep over the meadow; it is true, they had never been seen, but the sound of the bells and the unhappy bellowing of the flock, had been heard.

Rudy listened eagerly, but without any fear, for he did not even know what that was, and whilst he listened he thought he heard the ghost-like hollow bellowing! Yes, it became more and more distinct, the men heard it also, they stopped talking, listened and told Rudy he must not sleep.

It was the Föhn which blew, the powerful storm-wind, which rushes down the mountains into the valley and with its strength bends the trees, as if they were mere reeds, and lifts the wooden houses from one side of the river to the other, as if the move had been made on a chess-board.

After the lapse of an hour, they told Rudy that the storm had now blown over and that he might rest; with this license, fatigued by his march, he at once fell asleep.

They departed early in the morning; the sun showed Rudy new mountains, new glaciers and snow-fields; they had now reached Canton Valais and the other side of the mountain ridge which was visible at Grindelwald, but they were still far from the new home. Other chasms, precipices, pasture-grounds; forests and paths through the woods, unfolded themselves to the view; other houses, other human beings—but what human beings!

Deformed creatures, with unmeaning, fat, yellowish-white faces; with a large, ugly, fleshy lump on their necks; these were cretins who dragged themselves miserably along and gazed with their stupid eyes on the strangers who arrived among them. As for the women, the greatest number of them were frightful!

Were these the inhabitants of the new home?

FOOTNOTES:

[A] A humid south wind on the lakes of Switzerland, a fearful storm.

III. THE FATHER'S BROTHER.

The people in the uncle's house, looked, thank heaven, like those whom Rudy was accustomed to see. But one cretin was there, a poor silly lad, one of the many miserable creatures, who on account of their poverty and need, always make their home among the families of Canton Valais and remain with each but a couple of months. The wretched Saperli happened to be there when Rudy arrived.

Rudy's father's brother was still a vigorous hunter and was also a cooper by trade; his wife, a lively little person, had what is called a bird's face; her eyes resembled those of an eagle and she had a long neck entirely covered with down.

Everything was new to Rudy, the dress, manners and customs, yes, even the language, but that is soon acquired and understood by a child's ear. Here, they seemed to be better off, than in his grandfather's house; the dwelling rooms were larger, the walls looked gay with their chamois horns and highly polished rifles; over the door-way hung the picture of the blessed Virgin; alpine roses and a burning lamp stood before it.

His uncle, was as we have said before, one of the most famous chamois hunters in the neighborhood and also the most experienced and best guide.

Rudy was to be the pet of the household, although there already was one, an old deaf and blind dog, whom they could no longer use; but they remembered his many past services and he was looked upon as a member of the family and was to pass his old days in peace. Rudy patted the dog, but he would have nothing to do with strangers; Rudy did not long remain one, for he soon took firm hold both in house and heart.

"One is not badly off in Canton Valais," said his uncle, "we have the chamois, they do not die out so soon as the mountain goat! It is a great deal better here now, than in the old times; they may talk about their glory as much as they please. The present time is much better, for a hole has been made in the purse and light and air let into our quiet valley.

When old worn-out customs die away, something new springs forth!" said he. When uncle became talkative, he told of the years of his childhood and of his father's active time, when Valais was still a closed purse, as the people called it, and when it was filled with sick people and miserable cretins. French soldiers came, they were the right kind of doctors, they not only shot down the sickness but the men also.

"The Frenchmen can beat the stones until they surrender! they cut the Simplon-road out of the rocks—they have hewn out such a road, that I now can tell a three year old child to go to Italy! Keep to the highway, and a child may find his way there!" Then the uncle would sing a French song and cry hurrah for Napoleon Bonaparte.

Rudy now heard for the first time of France, of Lyons—the large city of the Rhone—for his uncle had been there.

"I wonder if Rudy will become an agile chamois hunter in a few years? He has every disposition for it!" said his uncle, and instructed him how to hold a rifle, how to aim and to fire. In the hunting season, he took him with him in the mountains and made him drink the warm chamois blood, which prevents the hunter from becoming dizzy. He taught him to heed the time when the avalanches roll down the different sides of the mountain—at mid-day or at night-fall —which depended upon the heat of the rays of the sun.

He taught him to notice the chamois, in order to learn from them how to jump, so as to alight steadily upon the feet. If there was no resting place in the clefts of the rock for the foot, he must know how to support himself with the elbow, and be able to climb by means of the muscles of the thigh and calf, even the neck must serve when it is necessary.

The chamois are cunning, they place out-guards—but the hunter must be still more cunning and follow the trail—and he can deceive them by hanging his coat and hat on his alpine stick, and so make the chamois take the coat for the man.

One day when Rudy was out with his uncle hunting, he tried this sport.

The rocky path was not wide; indeed there was scarcely any, only a narrow ledge, close to the dizzy abyss. The snow was half-thawed, the stones crumbled when trodden upon, and his uncle stretched himself out full length and crept along. Each stone as it broke away, fell, knocked itself, bounded and then rolled down; it made many leaps from one rocky wall to another until it found repose in the black deep.

Rudy stood about a hundred steps behind his uncle on the outermost cliff, and saw a huge golden vulture, hovering over his uncle, and sailing towards him through the air, as though wishing to cast the creeping worm into the abyss with one blow of his wing, and to make carrion of him. His uncle had only eyes for the chamois and its young kid, on the other side of the cleft. Rudy looked at the bird, understood what it wanted, and laid his hand on his rifle in order to shoot it. At that moment the chamois leaped—his uncle fired—the ball hit the animal, but the kid was gone, as though flight and danger had been its life's experience. The monstrous bird terrified by the report of the gun, took flight in another direction, and Rudy's uncle knew nought of his danger, until Rudy told him of it.

As they now were on their way home in the gayest spirits— his uncle playing one of his youthful melodies on his flute —they suddenly heard not far from them a singular sound; they looked sideways, they gazed aloof and saw high above them the snow covering of the rugged shelf of the rock, waving like an outspread piece of linen when agitated by the wind. The icy waves cracked like slabs of marble, they broke, dissolved in foaming, rushing water and sounded like a muffled thunder-clap. It was an avalanche rolling down, not over Rudy and his uncle, but near, only too near to them.

"Hold fast, Rudy," cried he, "firm, with your whole strength!"

And Rudy clasped the trunk of a tree; his uncle climbed into its branches and held fast, whilst the avalanche rolled many fathoms away from them. But the air-drift of the blustering storm, which accompanied it, bowed down the trees and bushes around them like dry reeds and threw them beyond. Rudy lay cast on the earth; the trunk of the tree on which he had held was as though sawed off, and its crown was hurled still farther along. His uncle lay amongst the broken branches, with his head shattered; his hands were yet warm, but his face was no longer to be recognized. Rudy stood pale and trembling; this was the first terror of his life, the first hour of fear that he had ever known.

Late in the evening, he returned with his message of death to his home, which was now one of sorrow.

The wife stood without words, without tears, and not until the corpse was brought home did her sorrow find an outburst. The poor cretin crept to his bed and was not seen all day, but towards evening he came to Rudy, and said: "Write a letter for me.

Saperli cannot write! Saperli can take the letter to the post office."

"A letter for you," asked Rudy, "and to whom?"

"To our Lord Christ!"

"What do you mean?"

And the half-witted creature gave a touching glance at Rudy, folded his hands and said piously and solemnly: "Jesus Christ! Saperli wishes to send him a letter, praying him to let Saperli lie dead and not the man of this house!"

And Rudy pressed his hand, "the letter cannot be sent, the letter will not give him back to us!"

It was difficult for Rudy to explain the impossibility to him.

"Now you are the stay of the house!" said his foster-mother, and Rudy became it.

IV. BABETTE.

Who is the best shot in Canton Valais? The chamois knew only too well: "Beware of Rudy!" they could say. Who is the handsomest hunter?— "It is Rudy." The young girls said this also, but they did not say: "Beware of Rudy!" No, not even the grave mothers, for he nodded to them quite as amicably as to the young girls. He was so bold and gay, his cheeks were brown, his teeth fresh and white and his coal-black eyes glittered; he was a handsome young fellow and but twenty years old. The icy water did not sting him when he swam, he could turn around in it like a fish; he could climb as did no one, and he was as firm on the rocky walls as a snail—for he had good sinews and muscles that served him well in leaping—the cat had first taught him this, and later the chamois.

One could not trust one's self to a better guide than to Rudy. In this way he could collect quite a fortune, but he had no taste for the trade of a cooper, which his uncle had taught him; his delight and pleasure was to shoot chamois, and this was profitable also. Rudy was a good match if one did not look higher than one's station, and in dancing he was just the kind of dancer that young girls dream about, and one or the other were always thinking of him when they were awake.

"He kissed me whilst dancing!" said the schoolmaster's Annette to her most intimate friend, but she should not have said this, not even to her dearest friend, but it is difficult to keep such things to one's self—like sand in a purse with a hole in it, it soon runs out—and although Rudy was so steady and good it was soon known that he kissed whilst dancing.

"Watch him," said an old hunter, "he has commenced with A, and he will kiss the whole alphabet through!"

A kiss, at a dance, was all they could say in their gossiping, but he had kissed Annette, and she was by no means the flower of his heart.

Down near Bex, between the great walnut trees, close by a rapid little stream, dwelt the rich miller. The dwelling-house was a large three-storied building, with little towers covered with wood and coated with sheets of lead, which shone in the sunshine and in the moonshine; the largest tower had for a weather-cock a bright arrow which pierced an apple and which was intended to represent the apple shot by Tell.

The mill looked neat and comfortable, so that it was really worth describing and drawing, but the miller's daughter could neither be described nor drawn, at least so said Rudy. Yet she was imprinted in his heart, and her eyes acted as a fire-brand upon it, and this had happened suddenly and un-expectedly. The most wonderful part of all was, that the miller's daughter, the pretty Babette, thought not of him, for she and Rudy had never even spoken two words with each other.

The miller was rich, and riches placed her much too high to be approached; "but no one," said Rudy to himself, "is placed so high as to be unapproachable; one must climb and one does not fall, when one does not think of it." *This* knowledge he had brought from home with him.

Now it so happened that Rudy had business at Bex and it was quite a journey there, for the railroad was not completed. The broad valley of Valais stretches itself from the glaciers of the Rhone, under the foot of the Simplon-mountain, between many varying mountain-heights, with its mighty river, the Rhone, which often swells and destroys everything, over-flooding fields and roads. The valley makes a bend, between the towns of Sion and St. Maurice, like an elbow and becomes so narrow at Maurice, that there only remains sufficient room for the river bed and a cart way.

Here an old tower stands like a sentry before the Canton Valais; it ends at this point and overlooks the bridge, which has a wall towards the custom-house. Now begins the Canton called Pays de Vaud and the nearest town is Bex, where everything becomes luxuriant and fruitful—one is in a garden of walnut and chestnut trees and here and there, cypress and pomegranate blossoms peep out—it is as warm as the South; one imagines one's self transplanted into Italy.

Rudy reached Bex, accomplished his business and looked about him, but he did not see a single miller's boy, not to speak of Babette. It appeared as though they were not to meet.

It was evening, the air was heavy with the wild thyme and blooming linden, a glistening veil lay over the forest-clad mountains, there was a stillness over everything, but not the quiet of sleep. It seemed as though all nature retained her breath, as if she felt disposed to allow her image to be imprinted upon the firmament.

Here and there, there were poles standing on the green fields, between the trees; they held the telegraph wire, which has been conducted through this peaceful valley. An object leant against one of these poles, so immoveable, that one might have taken it for a withered trunk of a tree; but it was Rudy. He slept not and still less was he dead; but as the most important events of this earth, as well as affairs of vital moment for individuals pass over the wires, without their giving out a tone or a tremulous movement, even so flashed through Rudy, thoughts—powerful, overwhelming, speaking of the happiness of his life; his, henceforth, "*constant thought.*"

His eyes were fixed upon a point in the trellis-work, and this was a light in Babette's sitting room. Rudy was so motionless, one might have thought that he was observing a chamois, in order to shoot it. Now, however, he was like the chamois—which appears sculptured on the rock, and suddenly if a stone rolls, springs and flies away—thus stood Rudy, until a thought struck him.

"Never despair," said he. "I shall make a visit to the mill, and say: Good evening miller, good evening Babette! One does not fall when one does not think of it! Babette must see me, if I am to be her husband!"

And Rudy laughed, was of good cheer and went to the mill; he knew what he wanted, he wanted Babette.

The river, with its yellowish white water rolled on; the willow trees and the lindens bowed themselves deep in the hastening water; Rudy went along the path, and as it says in the old child's song:

— — — — — — *Zu des Müllers Haus,*
Aber da war Niemand drinnen

Nur die Katze schaute aus![B]

The house-cat stood on the step, put up her back and said: "Meow!" but Rudy had no thoughts for her language, he knocked, no one heard, no one opened. "Meow!" said the cat. If Rudy had been little, he would have understood the speech of animals and known that the cat told him: "There is no one at home!" He was obliged to cross over to the mill, to make inquiries, and here he had news.

The master of the house was away on a journey, far away in the town of Interlaken—*inter lacus*, "between the lakes"—as the school-master, Annette's father, had explained, in his wisdom. Far away was the miller and Babette with him; there was to be a shooting festival, which was to commence on the following day and to continue for a whole week. The Swiss from all the German cantons were to meet there.

Poor Rudy, one could well say that he had not taken the happiest time to visit Bex; now he could return and that was what he did. He took the road over Sion and St. Maurice, back to his own valley, back to his own mountain, but he was not down-cast. On the following morning, when the sun rose, his good humor had returned, in fact it had never left him.

"Babette is in Interlaken, many a day's journey from here!" said he to himself, "it is a long road thither, if one goes by the highway, but not so far if one passes over the rocks and that is the road for a chamois hunter! I went this road formerly, for there is my home, where I lived with my grandfather when I was a little child, and they have a shooting festival in Interlaken! I will be the *first* one there, and that will I be with Babette also, as soon as I have made her acquaintance!"

With his light knapsack containing his Sunday clothes, with his gun and his huntsman's pouch, Rudy ascended the mountain. The short road, was a pretty long one, but the shooting-match had but commenced to-day and was to last more than a week; the miller and Babette were to remain the whole time, with their relations in Interlaken. Rudy crossed the Gemmi, for he wished to go to Grindelwald.

He stepped forwards merry and well, out into the fresh, light mountain air. The valley sank beneath him, the horizon widened; here and there a snow-peak, and soon appeared the whole shining white alpine chain. Rudy knew every snow mountain, onward he strode towards the Schreckhorn, that elevates its white powdered snow-finger high in the air.

At last he crossed the ridge of the mountain and the pasture-grounds and reached the valley of his home; the air was light and his spirits gay, mountain and valley stood resplendent with verdure and flowers. His heart was filled with youthful thoughts; — that one can never grow old, never die; but live, rule and enjoy; — free as a bird, light as a bird was he. The swallows flew by and sang as in his childhood: "We and you, and You and we!" All was happiness.

Below lay the velvet-green meadow, with its brown wooden houses, the Lütschine hummed and roared. He saw the glacier with its green glass edges and its black crevices in the deep snow, and the under and upper glacier. The sound of the church-bells was carried over to him, as if they chimed a welcome home; his heart beat loudly and expanded, so, that for a moment, Babette vanished from it; his heart widened, it was so full of recollections. He retraced his steps, over the path, where he used to stand when a little boy, with the other children, on the edge of the ditch, and where he sold carved wooden houses.

Yonder, under the fir-trees was his grandfather's house,—strangers dwelled there. Children came running up the path, wishing to sell; one of them held an alpine rose towards him. Rudy took it for a good omen and thought of Babette. Quickly he crossed the bridge, where the two Lütschines meet; the leafy trees had increased and the walnut trees gave deeper shade. He saw the streaming Swiss and Danish flags—the white cross on the red cloth—and Interlaken lay before him.

It was certainly a magnificent town; like no other, it seemed to Rudy. A Swiss town in its Sunday dress, was not like other trading-places, a mass of black stone houses, heavy, uninviting and stiff. No! it looked as though the wooden houses, on the mountain had run down into the green valley, to the clear, swift river and had ranged themselves in a row—a little in and out—so as to form a street, the most splendid of all streets, which had grown up since Rudy was here as a child.

It appeared to him, that here all the pretty wooden houses that his grandfather had carved, and with which the cupboard at home used to be filled, had placed themselves there and had grown in strength, as the old, the oldest chestnut trees had done. Each house had carved wood-work around the windows and balconies, projecting roofs, pretty and neat; in front of every house a little flower garden extended into the stone-covered street.

The houses were all placed on one side, as if they wished to conceal the forest-green meadow, where the cows with their tinkling bells made one fancy one's self near the high alpine pasture-grounds. The meadow was enclosed with high mountains, that leaned to one side so that the Jungfrau, the most stately of the Swiss mountains, with its glistening snow-clad top, was visible.

What a quantity of well dressed ladies and gentlemen from foreign countries! What multitudes of inhabitants from the different cantons! The shooters, with their numbers placed in a wreath around their hats, waiting to take their turn. Here was music and song, hurdy-gurdies and wind instruments, cries and confusion. The houses and bridges were decked with devices and verses; banners and flags floated, rifles sounded shot after shot; this was the best music to Rudy's ear and he entirely forgot Babette, although he had come for her sake.

The marksmen thronged towards the spot where the target-shooting was; Rudy was soon among them and he was the best, the luckiest, for he always hit the mark.

"Who can the strange hunter be?" they asked, "He speaks the French language as though he came from Canton Valais!" "He speaks our German very distinctly!" said others. "He is said to have lived in the neighborhood of Grindelwald, when a child!" said one of them.

There was life in the youth; his eyes sparkled, his aim was true. Good luck gives courage, and Rudy had courage at all times; he soon had a large circle of friends around him, they praised him, they did homage to him, and Babette had almost entirely left his thoughts. At that moment a heavy hand struck him on the shoulder, and a gruff voice addressed him in the French tongue:

"You are from Canton Valais?"

Rudy turned around. A stout person, with a red, contented countenance, stood by him and that was the rich miller of Bex. He covered with his wide body, the slight pretty Babette, who however, soon peeped out with her beaming dark eyes. The rich peasant became consequential because the hunter from his canton had made the best shot and was the honored one. Rudy was certainly a favorite of fortune, that, for which he had journeyed thither and almost forgotten had sought him.

When one meets a countryman far from one's home, why then one knows one another, and speaks together. Rudy was the first at the shooting festival and the miller was the first at Bex, through his money and mill, and so the two men pressed each other's hands: this they had never done before. Babette also, gave Rudy her little hand and he pressed her's in return and looked at her, so—that she became quite red.

The miller told of the long journey which they had made here, of the many large towns which they had seen—that was a real journey; they had come in the steam-boat and had been driven by post and rail!

"I came by the short road," said Rudy, "I came over the mountains; there is no path so high, that one can not reach it!"

"But one can break one's neck," said the miller, "you look as though you would do so some day, you are so daring!"

"One does not fall, when one does not think of it!" said Rudy.

And the miller's family in Interlaken, with whom the miller and Babette were staying, begged Rudy to pay them a visit, for he was from the same canton as their relations.

These were glad tidings for Rudy, fortune smiled upon him, as it always does on those that rely upon themselves and think upon the saying: "Our Lord gives us nuts, but he does not crack them for us!" Rudy made himself quite at home with the miller's relations; they drank the health of the best marksman. Babette knocked her glass against his and Rudy gave thanks for the honor shown him.

In the evening, they all walked under the walnut trees, in front of the decorated hôtels; there was such a crowd, such a throng, that Rudy was obliged to offer his arm to Babette. "He was so rejoiced to have met people from Pays de Vaud," said he, "Pays de Vaud and Valais were good neighborly cantons." His joy was so profound that it struck Babette, she must press his hand.

They walked along almost like old acquaintances; she was so amusing, the darling little creature, it became her so prettily Rudy thought, when she described what was laughable and overdone in the dress of the ladies, and ridiculed their manners and walk. She did not do this in order to mock them, for no doubt they were very good people, yes! kind and amiable.

Babette knew what was right, for she had a god-mother that was a distinguished English lady. She was in Bex, eighteen years ago, when Babette was baptized; she had given Babette, the expensive breast-pin which she wore. The god-mother had written her two letters; this year she was to meet her in Interlaken, with her daughters; they were old maids, over thirty years old, said Babette;—she was just eighteen.

The sweet little mouth was not still a minute; everything that Babette said, sounded to Rudy of great importance. Then he related how often he had been in Bex, how well he knew the mill; how often he had seen Babette, but she of course had never remarked him; he told how, when he reached the mill, with many thoughts to which he could give no utterance, she and her father were far away; still not so far as to render it impossible for him to ascend the rocky wall which made the road so long.

Yes, he said this; and he also said how much he thought of her; that it was for her sake and not on account of the shooting festival that he had come.

Babette remained very still, for what he confided to her was almost too much joy.

The sun set behind the rocky wall, whilst they were walking, and there stood the Jungfrau in all her radiant splendor, surrounded by the dark green circle of the adjacent mountains. The vast crowd of people stopped to look at it, Rudy and Babette also gazed upon its grandeur.

"It is nowhere more beautiful than here!" said Babette.

"Nowhere!" said Rudy, and looked at Babette.

"I must leave to-morrow!" said he, a little later.

"Visit us in Bex," whispered Babette, "it will delight my father!"

FOOTNOTES:

[B] The cat looked out from the miller's house,
No one was in, not even a mouse!

V. HOMEWARDS.

Ah! how much Rudy carried with him, as he went home the next morning over the mountains. Yes, there were three silver goblets, two very fine rifles and a silver coffee pot, which one could use if one wished to go to house-keeping; but he carried with him something far, far more important, far mightier, or rather *that* carried him over the high mountains.

The weather was raw, moist and cold, grey and heavy; the clouds lowered over the mountain-tops like mourning veils, and enveloped the shining peaks of the rocks. The sound of the axe resounded from the depths of the forest, and the trunks of the trees rolled down the mountain, looking in the distance like slight sticks, but on approaching them they were heavy trees, suitable for making masts. The Lütschine rushed on with its monotonous sound, the wind blustered, the clouds sailed by.

Suddenly a young girl approached Rudy, whom he had not noticed before; not until she was beside him; she also was about crossing the mountain. Her eyes had so peculiar a power that one was forced to look into them; they were so strangely clear—clear as glass, so deep, so fathomless—

"Have you a beloved one?" asked Rudy; for to have a beloved one was everything to him.

"I have none!" said she, and laughed; but it was as though she was not speaking the truth. "Do not let us take a by-way," continued she, "we must go more to the left, that way is shorter!"

"Yes, so as to fall down a precipice!" said Rudy; "Do you know no better way, and yet wish to be a guide?"

"I know the road well," said she, "my thoughts are with me; yours are beneath in the valley; here on high, one must think on the Ice-Maiden, for they say she is not well disposed to mankind!"

"I do not fear her," said Rudy, "she was forced to let me go when I was a child, so I suppose I can slip away from her now that I am older!"

The darkness increased, the rain fell, the snow came; it shone and dazzled. "Give me your hand, I will help you to ascend!" said the girl, and touched him with icy-cold fingers.

"You help me," said Rudy, "I do not yet need a woman's help in climbing!" He strode quickly on, away from her; the snow-shower formed a curtain around him, the wind whistled by him and he heard the young girl laugh and sing; it sounded so oddly! Yes, that was certainly a spirit in the service of the Ice-Maiden. Rudy had heard of them, when he had passed a night on high; when he had crossed the mountain, as a little boy.

The snow fell more scantily and the shadows lay under him; he looked back, there was no one to be seen, but he heard laughing and *jodling* and it did not appear to come from a human being. When Rudy reached the uppermost portion of the mountain, where the rocky path leads to the valley of the Rhone, he saw in the direction of Chamouni, two bright stars, twinkling and shining in the clear streaks of blue; he thought of Babette, of himself, of his happiness and became warmed by his thoughts.

VI. THE VISIT TO THE MILL.

"You bring princely things into the house!" said the old foster-mother, her singular eagle-eyes glistened and she made strange and hasty motions with her lean neck.

"Fortune is with you, Rudy, I must kiss you, my sweet boy!"

Rudy allowed himself to be kissed, but one could read in his countenance, that he but submitted to circumstances and to little household miseries. "How handsome you are, Rudy!" said the old woman.

"Do not put notions into my head!" answered Rudy, and laughed, but still it pleased him.

"I say it once more," said the old woman, "fortune is with you!"

"Yes, I agree with you there!" said he; thought of Babette and longed to be in the deep valley. "They must have returned, two days have passed since they expected to do so. I must go to Bex!"

Rudy went to Bex, and the inhabitants of the mill had returned; he was well received and they brought him greetings from the family at Interlaken. Babette did not talk much, she had grown silent; but her eyes spoke and that was quite enough for Rudy. The miller who generally liked to carry on the conversation—for he was accustomed to have every one laugh at his witty sayings and puns—was he not the rich miller?—seemed now to prefer to listen.

Rudy recounted to him his hunting expeditions; described the difficulties, the dangers and the privations of the chamois hunter when on the lofty mountain peak; how often he must climb over the insecure snow-ledges, that the wind had blown on the rocky brink, and how he must pass over slight bridges that the snow-drifts had thrown across the abyss.

Rudy looked fearless, his eyes sparkled whilst he spoke of the shrewdness of the chamois, of their daring leaps, of the violence of the Föhn and of the rolling avalanches. He observed that with every description he won more and more favor; but what pleased the miller more than all, was the account of the lamb's vulture and the bold golden eagle.

In Canton Valais, not far from here, there was an eagle's nest, very slyly built under the projecting edge of the rock; a young one was in it, but no one could steal it! An Englishman had offered Rudy a few days before, a whole handful of gold, if he would bring him the young one alive, "but everything has a limit," said he, "the young eagle cannot be taken away, and it would be madness to attempt it!"

The wine and conversation flowed freely; but the evening appeared all too short for Rudy; yet it was past midnight, when he went home from his first visit to the mill.

The light shone a little while longer through the window and between the green trees; the parlor-cat came out of an opening in the roof and the kitchen-cat came along the gutter.

"Do you know the latest news at the mill?" said the parlor-cat, "there has been a silent betrothal in the house! Father does not yet know it, but Rudy and Babette have reached each other their paws under the table, and he trod three times on my fore-paws, but still I did not mew, for that would have awakened attention!"

"I should have done it, nevertheless!" said the kitchen-cat.

"What is suited to the kitchen is not suited to the parlor," said the parlor-cat. "I should like to know what the miller will say, when he hears of the betrothal!"

Yes, what the miller would say! That was what Rudy would have liked to know, for Rudy was not at all patient. When the omnibus rumbled over the bridge of the Rhone, between Valais and Pays de Vaud not many days after, Rudy sat in it and was of good cheer; filled with pleasing thoughts of the "Yes," of the same evening.

When evening came and the omnibus returned, yes, there sat Rudy within, but the parlor-cat, was running about in the mill with great news.

"Listen, you, in the kitchen! The miller knows everything now. This has had an exquisite ending! Rudy came here towards evening; he and Babette had much to whisper and to chatter about, as they stood in the walk, under the miller's chamber. I lay close to their feet but they had neither eyes nor thoughts for me. 'I am going directly to your father,' said Rudy, 'this is an honorable affair!' 'Shall I follow you?' asked Babette, 'it may give you more courage!' 'I have courage enough,' said Rudy, 'but if you are there, he will be forced to look at it in a more favorable light!' They went in. Rudy trod heavily on my tail!

Rudy is indescribably awkward; I mewed, but neither he nor Babette had ears to hear it. They opened the door, they entered and I preceded them; I leaped upon the back of a chair, for I did not know but that Rudy would overturn everything! But the miller reversed all, that was a great step! Out of the door, up the mountains, to the chamois! Rudy can aim at them now, but not at our little Babette!"

"But what was said?" asked the kitchen-cat.

"Said? Everything. 'I care for her and she cares for me! When there is milk enough in the jug for one, there is milk enough in the jug for two!' 'But she is placed too high for you,' said the miller, 'she sits on gold dust, so now you know it; you can not reach her!' 'Nothing is too high; he who wills can reach anything!' said Rudy. He is too head-strong on this subject! 'But you cannot reach the eaglet, you said so yourself lately! Babette is still higher!' 'I will have them both!' said Rudy. 'Yes, I will bestow her upon you, if you make me a present of the eaglet alive!' said the miller and laughed until the tears stood in his eyes.

"'Thanks for your visit, Rudy! Come again to-morrow, you will find no one at home. Farewell, Rudy!' Babette said farewell also, as sorrowfully as a kitten, that cannot see its mother. 'A word is a word, a man is a man,' said Rudy, 'do not weep Babette, I shall bring the eaglet!' 'I hope that you will break your neck!' said the miller. That's what I call an overturning! Now Rudy has gone, and Babette sits and weeps; but the miller sings in German, he learned to do so whilst on his journey! I do not intend to trouble myself any longer about it, it does no good!"

"There is still a prospect!" said the kitchen-cat.

VII. THE EAGLE'S NEST.

Merry and loud sounded the *jodel* from the mountain-path, it indicated good humor and joyous courage; it was Rudy; he was going to his friend Vesinand.

"You must help me! We will take Ragli with us; I am going after the eaglet on the brink of the rock!"

"Do you not wish to go after the black spot in the moon? That is quite as easy," said Vesinand; "you are in a good humor!"

"Yes, because I am thinking of my wedding; but seriously, you shall know how my affairs stand!"

Vesinand and Ragli soon knew what Rudy wished.

"You are a bold fellow," said they, "do not do this! You will break your neck!"

"One does not fall, when one does not think of it!" said Rudy.

About mid-day, they set out with poles, ladders and ropes; their path lay through bushes and brambles, over the rolling stones, up, up in the dark night.

The water rushed beneath them; the water flowed above them and the humid clouds chased each other in the air. The hunters approached the steep brink of the rock; it became darker and darker, the rocky walls almost met; high above them in the narrow fissure the air penetrated and gave light. Under their feet there was a deep abyss with its roaring waters.

They all three sat still, awaiting the grey of the morning; then the eagle would fly out; they must shoot him before they could think of obtaining the young one. Rudy seemed

116

to be a part of the stone on which he sat; his rifle placed before him, ready to take aim, his eyes immovably fastened on yon high cleft which concealed the eagle's nest. The three huntsmen waited long.

A crashing, whizzing noise sounded high above them; a large hovering object darkened the air. Two rifle barrels were aimed as the black eagle flew from its nest; a shot was heard, the out-spread wings moved an instant, then the bird slowly sank as if it wished to fill the entire cliff with its outstretched wings and bury the huntsmen in its fall. The eagle sank in the deep; the branches of the trees and bushes cracked, broken by the fall of the bird.

They now displayed their activity; three of the longest ladders were tied together; they stood them on the farthest point where the foot could place itself with security, close to the brink of the precipice—but they were not long enough; there was still a great space from the outermost projecting cliff, which protected the nest; the rocky wall was perfectly smooth. After some consultation, they decided to lower into the opening two ladders tied together and to fasten them to the three already beneath them. With great difficulty they dragged them up and attached them with cords; the ladders shot over the projecting cliffs and hung over the chasm; Rudy sat already on the lowest round.

It was an ice-cold morning, and the mist mounted from the black ravine. Rudy sat there like a fly on a rocking blade of grass, which a nest-building bird has dropped in its hasty flight, on the edge of a factory chimney; but the fly had the advantage of escaping by its wings, poor Rudy had none, he was almost sure to break his neck. The wind whistled around him and the roaring water from the thawed glaciers, the palace of the Ice-Maiden, poured itself into the abyss.

He gave the ladders a swinging motion—as the spider swings herself by her long thread—he seized them with a strong and steady hand, but they shook as if they had worn-out hasps.

The five long ladders looked like a tremulous reed, as they reached the nest and hung perpendicularly over the rocky wall. Now came the most dangerous part; Rudy had to climb as a cat climbs; but Rudy could do this, for the cat had taught it to him. He did not feel that Vertigo trod in the air behind him and stretched her polypus-like arms towards him. Now he stood on the highest round of the ladder and perceived that he was not sufficiently high to enable him to see into the nest; he could reach it with his hands.

He tried how firm the twigs were, which plaited in one another formed the bottom of the nest; when he had assured himself of a thick and immoveable one, he swung himself off of the ladder. He had his breast and head over the nest, out of which streamed towards him a stifling stench of carrion; torn lambs, chamois and birds lay decomposing around him. Vertigo, who had no power over him, blew poisonous vapors into his face to stupefy him; below in the black, yawning abyss, sat the Ice-Maiden herself, on the hastening water, with her long greenish-white hair and stared at him with death-like eyes, which were pointed at him like two rifle barrels.

"Now, I shall catch you!"

Seated in one corner of the eagle's nest was the eaglet, who could not fly yet, although so strong and powerful. Rudy fastened his eyes on it, held himself with his whole strength firmly by one hand, and with the other threw the noose around it. It was captured alive, its legs were in the knot; Rudy cast the rope over his shoulder, so that the animal dangled some distance below him, and sustained himself by another rope which hung down, until his feet touched the upper round of the ladder.

"Hold fast, do not think that you will fall and then you are sure not to do so!" That was the old lesson, and he followed it; held fast, climbed, was sure not to fall and he did not.

There resounded a strong *jodling*, and a joyous one too. Rudy stood on the firm, rocky ground with the young eaglet.

VIII. THE NEWS WHICH THE PARLOR-CAT RELATED.

"Here is what you demanded!" said Rudy, on entering the house of the miller at Bex, as he placed a large basket on the floor and took off the covering. Two yellow eyes, with black circles around them, fiery and wild, looked out as if they wished to set on fire, or to kill those around them. The short beak yawned ready to bite and the neck was red and downy.

"The eaglet!" cried the miller. Babette screamed, jumped to one side and could neither turn her eyes from Rudy, nor from the eaglet.

"You do not allow yourself to be frightened!" said the miller.

"And you keep your word, at all times," said Rudy, "each has his characteristic trait!"

119

"But why did you not break your neck?" asked the miller.

"Because I held on firmly," answered Rudy, "and I hold firmly on Babette!"

"First see that you have her!" said the miller and laughed; that was a good sign; Babette knew this.

"Let us take the eaglet from the basket, it is terrible to see how he glares! How did you get him?"

Rudy was obliged to recount his adventure, whilst the miller stared at him with eyes, which grew larger and larger.

"With your courage and with your luck you could take care of three wives!" said the miller.

"Thanks! Thanks!" cried Rudy.

"Yes, but you have not yet Babette!" said the miller as he struck the young chamois hunter, jestingly on the shoulder.

"Do you know the latest news in the mill?" said the parlor-cat to the kitchen-cat. "Rudy has brought us the young eagle and taken Babette in exchange. They have kissed each other and the father looked on. That is just as good as a betrothal; the old man did not overturn anything, he drew in his claws, took his nap and left the two seated, caressing each other. They have so much to relate, they will not get through till Christmas!"

They had not finished at Christmas.

The wind whistled through the brown foliage, the snow swept through the valley as it did on the high mountains. The Ice-Maiden sat in her proud castle and arrayed herself in her winter costume; the ice walls stood in glazed frost; where the mountain streams waved their watery veil in summer, were now seen thick elephantine icicles, shining garlands of ice, formed of fantastic ice crystals, encircled the fir-trees, which were powdered with snow.

The Ice-Maiden rode on the blustering wind over the deepest valleys. The snow covering lay over all Bex; Rudy stayed in doors more than was his wont, and sat with Babette. The wedding was to take place in the summer; their friends talked so much of it that it often made their ears burn. All was sunshine with them, and the loveliest alpine rose was Babette, the sprightly, laughing Babette, who was as charming as the early spring; the spring that makes the birds sing, that will bring the summer time and the wedding day.

"How can they sit there and hang over each other," exclaimed the parlor-cat, "I am really tired of their eternal mewing!"

IX. THE ICE-MAIDEN.

The early spring time had unfolded the green leaves of the walnut and chestnut trees; they were remarkably luxuriant from the bridge of St. Maurice to the banks of the lake of Geneva.

The Rhone, which rushes forth from its source, has under the green glacier the palace of the Ice-Maiden. She is carried by it and the sharp wind to the elevated snow-fields, where she extends herself on her damp cushions in the brilliant sunshine. There she sits and gazes, with far-seeing sight, upon the valley where mortals busily move about like so many ants.

"Beings endowed with mental powers, as the children of the Sun, call you," said the Ice-Maiden—"ye are worms! *One* snow-ball rolled and you and your houses and towns are crushed and swept away!" She raised her proud head still higher and looked with death-beaming eyes far around and below her. From the valley resounded a rumbling, a blasting of rocks, men were making railways and tunnels. "They are playing like moles," said she, "they excavate passages, and a noise is made like the firing of a gun. When I transpose *my* castles, it roars louder than the rolling of the thunder!"

A smoke arose from the valley and moved along like a floating veil, like a waving plume; it was the locomotive which led the train over the newly built railroad—this crooked snake, whose limbs are formed of cars upon cars. It shot along with the speed of an arrow.

"They are playing the masters with their mental powers," said the Ice-Maiden, "but the powers of nature are the ruling ones!" and she laughed and her laugh was echoed in the valley.

"Now an avalanche is rolling!" said the men below.

Still more loudly sang the children of the Sun; they sang of the "thoughts" of men which fetter the sea to the yoke, cut down mountains and fill up valleys; of human thoughts which rule the powers of nature. At this moment, a company of travelers crossed the snow-field where the Maiden sat; they had bound themselves firmly together with ropes, in order to form a large body on the smooth ice-field by the deep abyss.

"Worms!" said she, "as if you were lords of creation!" She turned from them and looked mockingly upon the deep valley, where the cars were rushing by.

"There sit those *thoughts* in their power of strength! I see them all!—There sits one, proud as a king and alone! They sit in masses! There, half are asleep! When the steam-dragon stops, they will descend and go their way! The thoughts go out into the world!" She laughed.

"There rolls another avalanche!" they said in the valley.

"It will not catch us!" said two on the back of the steam dragon;—"two souls and one thought"—these were Rudy and Babette; the miller was there also.

"As baggage," said he, "I go along, as the indispensable!"

"There sit the two," said the Ice-Maiden, "I have crushed many a chamois; I have bent and broken millions of alpine roses, so that no roots were left! I shall annihilate *them*! The thoughts! The mental powers!" She laughed.

"There rolls another avalanche!" they said in the valley.

X. THE GOD-MOTHER.

In Montreux, one of the adjoining towns, which with Clarens, Vernex and Crin forms a garland around the north-

123

east part of the lake of Geneva, dwelt Babette's god-mother, a distinguished English lady, with her daughters and a young relation. Although she had but lately arrived, the miller had already made her his visit and announced Babette's engagement; had spoken of Rudy and the eaglet; of the visit to Interlaken and in short had told the whole story. This had rejoiced her in the highest degree, both for Rudy and Babette's sake, as well as for the miller's; they must all visit her—therefore they came. Babette was to see her god-mother, and the god-mother was to see Babette.

At the end of the lake of Geneva, by the little town of Villeneuve, lay the steam-boat which after half an hour's trip from Vernex, arrived at Montreux. This is one of the coasts which are sung of by the poets. Here sat Byron, by the deep bluish green lake, under the walnut trees and wrote his melodious verses upon the prisoner of the deep sombre castle of Chillon.

Here, where Clarens with its weeping willows, mirrored itself in the waters, once wandered Rousseau and dreamt of Heloïse. Yonder, where the Rhone glides along under Savoy's snow-topped mountains and not far from its mouth, in the lake lies a little island, indeed it is so small, that from the coast it is taken for a vessel. It is a valley between the rocks, which a lady caused to be dammed up a hundred years ago and to be covered with earth and planted with three acacia-trees, which now shade the whole island. Babette was quite charmed with this little spot; they must and should go there, yes, it must be charming beyond description to be on the island; but the steamer sailed by, and stopped as it should, at Vernex.

The little party wandered between the white, sunlit walls, which surround the vineyards of the little mountain town of Montreux, through the fig-trees which flourish before every peasant's house and in whose gardens, the laurel and cypress trees are green. Half-way up the hill stood the boarding house where the god-mother resided.

The reception was very cordial. The god-mother was a large amiable person and had a round smiling countenance; as a child she must have had a real Raphael's angel head, but now it was an old angel's head with silvery white hair, well curled. The daughters were tall, slender, refined and much dressed. The young cousin who was with them, was clad in white from head to foot; he had golden hair and immense whiskers; he immediately showed little Babette the greatest attention.

Richly bound books, loose music and drawings lay strewn about the large table; the balcony door stood open and one had a view of the beautiful out-spread lake, which was so shining, so still, that the mountains of Savoy with their little villages, their forest and their snowy peaks mirrored themselves in it.

Rudy, who usually was so full of life, so merry and so daring, did not feel in his element; he moved about over the smooth floor as though he were treading on peas. How wearily the time dragged along, it was just as if one was in a tread mill! If they did go walking, why, that was just as slow; Rudy could take two steps forwards and two steps backwards and still remain in the pace of the others.

When they came to Chillon, (the old sombre castle on the rocky island) they entered in order to see the dungeon and the martyr's stake, as well as the rusty chains on the wall; the stone bed for those condemned to death and the trap-door where the wretched beings impaled on iron goads, were hurled into the breakers. It was a place of execution elevated through Byron's song to the world of poetry.

Rudy was sad, he lent over the broad stone sill of the window, gazed into the deep blue water and over to the little solitary island with its three acacias and wished himself there, free from the whole gossiping society. Babette was remarkably merry, she had been indescribably amused. The cousin found her perfect.

"Yes, a perfect jackanapes!" said Rudy; this was the first time, that he had said something, that did not please her. The Englishman had presented her with a little book, as a souvenir of Chillon,—Byron's poem of "The Prisoner of Chillon," in the French language, so that Babette might read it.

"The book may be good," said Rudy, "but the finely combed fellow that gave it to you does not please me!"

"He looked like a meal-bag, without meal in it!" said the miller and laughed at his own wit. Rudy laughed and thought that this was very well said.

XI. THE COUSIN.

When Rudy came to the mill, a couple of days afterwards, he found the young Englishman there. Babette had just cooked some trout for him and had dressed them with parsley in order to make them appear more inviting. That was assuredly not necessary. What did the Englishman want here? Did he come in order to have Babette entertain and wait upon him?

Rudy was jealous and that amused Babette; it rejoiced her, to learn the feelings of his heart, the strong as well as the weak ones.

Until now love had been a play and she played with Rudy's whole heart; yet he was her happiness, her life's thought, the noblest one! The more gloomy he looked, the more her eyes laughed and she would have liked to kiss the blonde Englishman with his golden whiskers, if she could have succeeded by so doing, in making Rudy rush away furious. Then, yes then, she would have known how much he loved her. That was not right, that was not wise in little Babette; but she was only nineteen! She did not reflect and still less did she think how her behavior towards the young Englishman might be interpreted; for it was lighter and merrier than was seemly for the honorable and newly affianced daughter of the miller.

The mill lay where the highway slopes—under the snow covered rocky heights—which are called here, in the language of the country "Diablerets" close to a rapid mountain stream, which was of a grayish white, like bubbling soap suds. A smaller stream, rushes forth from the rocks on the other side of the river, passes through an enclosed, broad rafter-made-gutter and turns the large wheel of the mill. The gutter was so full of water, that it streamed over and offered a most slippery way, to one who had the idea of crossing more quickly to the mill; a young man had this idea—the Englishman.

Guided by the light, which shone from Babette's window, he arrived in the evening, clothed in white, like a miller's boy; he had not learnt to climb and nearly tumbled head over heels into the stream, but escaped with wet sleeves and splashed pantaloons. He reached Babette's window, muddy and wet through, there he climbed into the old linden tree and imitated the screech of an owl, for he could not sing like any other bird. Babette heard it and peeped through the thin curtains, but when she remarked the white man and recognized him, her little heart fluttered with alarm, but also with anger. She hastily extinguished the light, fastened the windows securely and then she let him howl.

If Rudy was in the mill it would have been dreadful, but Rudy was not there; no, it was much worse, for he was below. There was loud conversation, angry words; there might be blows; yes, perhaps murder.

Babette was terrified; she opened the window, called Rudy's name and begged him to go; she said she would not suffer him to remain.

"You will not suffer me to remain," he exclaimed, "then it is a preconcerted thing! You were expecting other friends, friends better than myself; shame on you, Babette!"

"You are detestable," said Babette, "I hate you!" and she wept. "Go! Go!"

"I have not deserved this!" said he, and departed. His cheeks burned like fire, his heart burned like fire.

Babette threw herself on her bed and wept.

"So much as I love you, Rudy, how can you believe ill of me!"

She was angry, very angry, and this was good for her; otherwise she would have sorrowed deeply; but now she could sleep, and she slept the strengthening sleep of youth.

XII. THE EVIL POWERS.

Rudy forsook Bex and went on his way home, in the fresh, cool air, up the snow-covered mountain, where the Ice-Maiden ruled. The leafy trees which lay beneath him, looked like potato vines; fir-trees and bushes became less frequent; the alpine roses grew in the snow, which lay in little spots like linen put out to bleach. There stood a blue anemone, he crushed it with the barrel of his gun.

Higher up two chamois appeared and Rudy's eyes gained luster and his thoughts took a new direction; but he was not near enough to make a good shot; he ascended still higher, where only stiff grass grows between the blocks of stone; the chamois were quietly crossing the snow field; he hurried hastily on; the fog was descending and he suddenly stood before the steep rocky wall. The rain commenced to fall.

He felt a burning thirst; heat in his head, cold in all his limbs; he grasped his hunting flask, but it was empty; he had not thought of filling it when he rushed up the hill. He had never been ill, but now he was so; he was weary and had a desire to throw himself down to sleep, but everything was streaming with water. He endeavored to collect his ideas, but all objects danced before his eyes. Suddenly he perceived a newly built house leaning against the rocks and in the doorway stood a young girl. Yes, it appeared to him that it was the schoolmaster's Annette, whom he had once kissed whilst dancing; but it was not Annette and yet he had seen her before — perhaps in Grindelwald, on the evening when he returned from the shooting-festival at Interlaken.

"Where do you come from?" asked he.

"I am at home," said she, "I tend my flock!"

"Your flock, where do they pasture? Here are only cliffs and snow!"

"You have a ready answer," said she and laughed; "below there is a charming meadow! There are my goats! I take good care of them! I lose none of them, what is mine, remains mine!"

"You are bold!" said Rudy.

"So are you!" answered she.

"Have you any milk? Do give me some, my thirst is intolerable!"

"I have something better than milk," said she, "and you shall have it!

Travelers came yesterday with their guide, but they forgot a flask of wine, such as you have never tasted; they will not come for it, I shall not drink it, so drink you!"

She brought the wine, poured it in a wooden cup and handed it to Rudy.

"That is good," said he, "I have never drunk such a warming, such a fiery wine!" His eyes beamed, a life, a glow came over him; all sorrow and oppression seemed to die away; gushing, fresh human nature stirred itself within him.

"Why this is the schoolmaster's Annette," exclaimed he, "give me a kiss!"

"Yes, give me the beautiful ring, which you wear on your finger!"

"My engagement ring?"

"Just that one!" said the young girl and pouring wine into the cup, put it to his lips and he drank. Then the joy of life streamed in his blood; the whole world seemed to belong to him. "Why torment one's self? Every thing is made for our enjoyment and happiness! The stream of life is the stream of joy, and forgetfulness is felicity!" He looked at the young girl, it was Annette and then again not Annette; still less, an enchanted phantom, as he had named her, when he met her near Grindelwald.

The girl on the mountain was fresh as the newly fallen snow, blooming as the alpine rose and light as a kid; and a human being like Rudy. He wound his arm about her, looked in her strange clear eyes, yes, only for a second— but was it spiritual life or was it death which flowed through him? Was he raised on high, or did he sink into the deep, murderous ice-pit, deeper and ever deeper? He saw icy walls like bluish green glass, numberless clefts yawned around, and the water sounded as it dropped, like a chime of bells; it was pearly, clear and shone in bluish white flames.

The Ice-Maiden gave him a kiss, which made him shiver from head to foot and he gave a cry of pain. He staggered and fell; it grew dark before his eyes, but soon all became clear to him again; the evil powers had had their sport with him.

The alpine maiden had vanished, the mountain hut had vanished, the water beat against the bare rocky walls and all around him lay snow. Rudy wet to the skin, trembled from

131

cold and his ring had disappeared, his engagement ring, which Babette had given him. He tried to fire off his rifle which lay near him in the snow but it missed. Humid clouds lay in the clefts like firm masses of snow and Vertigo watched for her powerless prey; beneath him in the deep chasm it sounded as if a block of the rock was rolling down and was endeavoring to crush and tear up all that met it in its fall.

In the mill sat Babette and wept; Rudy had not been there for six days; he who had been so wrong; he who must beg her forgiveness, because she loved him with her whole heart.

XIII. IN THE MILLER'S HOUSE.

"What confusion!" said the parlor-cat to the kitchen-cat.

"Now all is wrong between Rudy and Babette. She sits and weeps and he thinks no longer on her, I suppose.

"I cannot bear it!" said the kitchen-cat.

"Nor I," said the parlor-cat, "but I shall not worry myself any longer about it! Babette can take the red-whiskered one for a dear one, but he has not been here either, since he tried to get on the roof!"

Within and without, the evil powers ruled, and Rudy knew this, and reflected upon what had taken place both around and within him, whilst upon the mountain.

Were those faces, or was all a feverish dream? He had never known fever or sickness before. Whilst he condemned Babette, he also condemned himself. He thought of the wild, wicked feelings which had lately possessed him. Could he confess everything to Babette? Every thought, which in the hour of temptation might have become a reality?

He had lost her ring and by this loss had she won him back. Could she confess to him? It seemed as if his heart would break when he thought of her; so many recollections passed through his soul. He saw her a lively, laughing, petulant child; many a loving word, which she had said to him in the fullness of her heart, shot like a sunbeam through his breast and soon all there was sunshine for Babette.

She must be able to confess to him and she should do so.

He came to the mill, he came to confession; and this commenced with a kiss, and ended with the fact that Rudy was the sinner; his great fault was, that he had doubted Babette's fidelity; yes, that was indeed atrocious in him! Such mistrust, such violence could bring them both into misfortune! Yes, most surely! Thereupon Babette preached him a little sermon, which much diverted her and became her charmingly; in one article Rudy was quite right; the god-mother's relation was a jackanapes! She should burn the book that he had given her, and not possess the slightest object which could remind her of him.

"Now it is all arranged," said the parlor-cat, "Rudy is here again, they understand each other and that is a great happiness!"

"Last night," said the kitchen-cat, "I heard the rats say that the greatest happiness was to eat tallow candles, and to

have abundance of tainted meat. Now who must one believe, the rats or the lovers?"

"Neither of them," said the parlor-cat, "that is the surest
way!"

The greatest happiness for Rudy and Babette was drawing
near; they were awaiting, so they said, their happiest day,
their wedding day.

But the wedding was not to be in the church of Bex, nor in
the miller's house; the god-mother wished it to be solem-
nized near her, and the marriage ceremony was to take
place in the beautiful little church of Montreux. The miller
insisted that her desire should be fulfilled; he alone knew
what the god-mother intended for the young couple; they
were to receive a bridal present from her, which was well
worth so slight a concession. The day was appointed. They
were to leave for Villeneuve, in time to arrive at Montreux
early in the morning, and so enable the god-mother's
daughters to dress the bride.

"Then I suppose there will be a wedding here in the house,
on the following day," said the parlor-cat, "otherwise, I
would not give a single mew for the whole thing!"

"There will be a feast here," said the kitchen-cat, "the ducks
are slain, the pigeons necks wrung, and a whole deer hangs
on the wall. My teeth itch just with looking on! To-morrow
the journey commences!"

Yes, to-morrow! Rudy and Babette sat together for the last
time in the mill.

Without was the alpine glow; the evening bells pealed; the
daughters of the Sun sang: "What is for the best will take
place!"

XIV. THE VISIONS OF THE NIGHT.

The sun had gone down; the clouds lowered themselves into the Rhone valley—between the high mountains; the wind blew from the south over the mountains—an African wind, a Föhn,—which tore the clouds asunder. When the wind had passed, all was still for an instant; the parted clouds hung in fantastic forms between the forest-grown mountains.

Over the hastening Rhone, their shapes resembled sea-monsters of the primeval world, soaring eagles of the air and leaping frogs of the ditches—they seemed to sink into the rapid stream and to sail on the river, yet they still floated in the air.

The stream carried away a pine tree, torn up by the roots; and the water sent whirlpools ahead; this was Vertigo, with her attendants, and they danced in circles on the foaming stream. The moon shone on the snow of the mountain-peaks; it lighted up the dark forest and the singular white clouds; the peasants of the mountain, saw through their window panes, the nightly apparitions and the spirits of the powers of nature, as they sailed before the Ice-Maiden. She came from her glacier castle, she sat in a frail bark, a felled fir-tree; the water of the glaciers carried her up the stream out to the main sea.

"The wedding guests are coming!" was whizzed and sung in the air and in the water.

Visions without and visions within!

Babette dreamt a wonderful dream.

It appeared to her, as though she was married to Rudy, and had been so for many years. He had gone chamois hunting and as she sat at home, the young Englishman with the golden whiskers was beside her; his eyes were fiery, his words seemed endowed with magical power; he reached her his hand and she was obliged to follow him.

They flew from home. Steadily downwards.

A weight lay upon her heart and it grew ever heavier. It was a sin against Rudy, a sin against God; suddenly she stood forsaken. Her clothes were torn by the thorns; her hair had grown grey; she looked up in her sorrow and she saw Rudy on the edge of the rock. She stretched her arms towards him, but she ventured neither to call, nor to implore him; but she soon saw that it was not he himself, only his hunting coat and hat, which were hanging on his alpine staff, as the hunters are accustomed to place them, in order to deceive the chamois! Babette moaned in boundless anguish:

"Ah! would that I had died on my wedding day, my happiest day! Oh! my heavenly Father! That would have been a mercy, a life's happiness! Then we would have obtained, the best, that could have happened to us! No one knows his future!" In her impious sorrow, she threw herself down the steep precipice. It seemed as if a string broke, and a sorrowful tone resounded.

Babette awoke—the dream was at an end and obliterated; but she knew that she had dreamt of something terrible, and of the young Englishman, whom she had neither seen, nor thought of, for many months.

Was he perhaps in Montreux? Should she see him at her
wedding? A slight shadow flitted over her delicate mouth,
her brow contracted; but her smile soon returned; her eyes
sparkled again; the sun shone so beautifully without, and
to-morrow, yes to-morrow was her and Rudy's wedding
day.

Rudy had already arrived, when she came down stairs, and
they soon left for Villeneuve. They were so happy, the two,
and the miller also; he laughed and was radiant with joy; he
was a good father, an honest soul.

"Now we are the masters of the house!" said the parlor-cat.

XV. CONCLUSION.

It was not yet night, when the three joyous people reached
Villeneuve and took their dinner. The miller seated himself
in an arm-chair with his pipe and took a little nap. The betrothed went out of the town arm in arm, out on the carriage
way, under the bush-grown rocks, to the deep bluish-green
lake. Sombre Chillon, with its grey walls and heavy towers,
mirrored itself in the clear water; but still nearer lay the little island, with its three acacias, and it looked like a bou-
quet on the lake.

"How charming it must be there!" said Babette; she felt
again the greatest desire to visit it, and this wish could be
immediately fulfilled; for a boat lay on the shore and the
rope which fastened it, was easy to untie. As no one was
visible, from whom they could ask permission, they took
the boat without hesitation, for Rudy could row well. The

oars skimmed like the fins of a fish, over the pliant water, which is so yielding and still so strong; which is all back to carry, but all mouth to engulf; which smiles—yes, is gentleness itself, and still awakens terror—and is so powerful in destroying. The rapid current soon brought the boat to the island; they stepped on land. There was just room enough for the two to dance.

Rudy swung Babette three times around, and then they seated themselves on the little bench, under the acacias, looked into each other's eyes, held each other by the hand, and everything around them shone in the splendor of the setting sun. The forests of fir-trees on the mountains became of a pinkish lilac aspect, the color of blooming heath, and where the bare rocks were apparent, they glowed as if they were transparent.

The clouds in the sky were radiant with a red glow; the whole lake was like a fresh flaming rose leaf. As the shadows arose to the snow-covered mountains of Savoy, they became dark blue, but the uppermost peak seemed like red lava and pointed out for a moment, the whole range of mountains, whose masses arose glowing from the bosom of the earth.

It seemed to Rudy and Babette, that they had never seen such an alpine glow. The snow-covered Dent-du-Midi, had a luster like the full moon, when it rises to the horizon.

"So much beauty, so much happiness!" they both said.

"Earth can give me no more," said Rudy, "an evening hour like this is a whole life! How often have I felt as now, and thought that if everything should end suddenly, how happily have I lived! How blessed is this world! The day ended, a new one dawned and I felt that it was still more beautiful! How bountiful is our Lord, Babette!"

"I am so happy!" said she.

"Earth can give me no more!" exclaimed Rudy.

The evening bells resounded from the Savoy and Swiss mountains; the bluish-black Jura arose in golden splendor towards the west.

"God give you that which is most excellent and best, Rudy!" said Babette.

"He will do that," answered Rudy, "to-morrow I shall have it! To-morrow you will be entirely mine! Mine own, little, lovely wife!"

"The boat!" cried Babette at the same moment.

The boat, which was to convey them back, had broken loose and was sailing from the island.

"I will go for it!" said Rudy. He threw off his coat, drew off his boots, sprang in the lake and swam towards the boat.

The clear, bluish-grey water of the ice mountains, was cold and deep. Rudy gave but a single glance and it seemed as though he saw a gold ring, rolling, shining and sporting— he thought on his lost engagement ring—and the ring grew larger, widened into a sparkling circle and within it shone the clear glacier; all about yawned endless deep chasms; the water dropped and sounded like a chime of bells, and shone with bluish-white flames. He saw in a second, what we must say in many long words.

Young hunters and young girls, men and women, who had once perished in the glacier, stood there living, with open eyes and smiling mouth; deep below them chimed from buried towns the peal of church bells; under the arches of the churches knelt the congregation; pieces of ice formed the organ pipes, and the mountain stream played the organ. On the clear transparent ground sat the Ice-Maiden; she raised herself towards Rudy, kissed his feet, and the coldness of death ran through his limbs and gave him an electric shock—ice and fire. He could not perceive the difference.

"Mine, mine!" sounded around him and within him.

"I kissed you, when you were young, kissed you on your mouth! Now I kiss your feet, you are entirely mine!"

He vanished in the clear blue water.

Everything was still; the church bells stopped ringing; the last tones died away with the splendor of the red clouds.

"You are mine!" sounded in the deep. "You are mine!" sounded from on high, from the infinite.

How happy to fly from love to love, from earth to heaven!

A string broke, a cry of grief was heard, the icy kiss of death conquered; the prelude ended; so that the drama of life might commence, discord melted into harmony.—

Do you call this a sad story?

Poor Babette! For her it was a period of anguish.

The boat drifted farther and farther. No one on shore knew that the lovers were on the island. The evening darkened, the clouds lowered themselves; night came. She stood there, solitary, despairing, moaning. A flash of lightning passed over the Jura mountains, over Switzerland and over Savoy. From all sides flash upon flash of lightning, clap upon clap of thunder, which rolled continuously many minutes.

At times the lightning was vivid as sunshine, and you could distinguish the grape vines; then all became black again in the dark night. The lightning formed knots, ties, zigzags, complicated figures; it struck in the lake, so that it lit it up on all sides; whilst the noise of the thunder was made louder by the echo. The boat was drawn on shore; all living objects sought shelter. Now the rain streamed down.

"Where can Rudy and Babette be in this frightful weather!" said the miller.

Babette sat with folded hands, with her head in her lap, mute with sorrow, with screaming and bewailing.

"In the deep water," said she to herself, "he is as far down as the glaciers!"

She remembered what Rudy had related to her of his mother's death, of his preservation, and how he was withdrawn death-like, from the clefts of the glacier. "The Ice-Maiden has him again!"

There was a flash of lightning, as dazzling as the sunlight on the white snow. Babette started up; at this instant, the sea rose like a glittering glacier; there stood the Ice-Maiden majestic, pale, blue, shining, and at her feet lay Rudy's corpse. "Mine!" said she, and then all around was fog and night and streaming water.

"Cruel!" moaned Babette, "why must he die, now that the day of our happiness approached. God! Enlighten my understanding! Enlighten my heart! I do not understand thy ways! Notwithstanding all thy omnipotence and wisdom, I still grope in the darkness."

God enlightened her heart. A thought like a ray of mercy, her last night's dream in all its vividness flashed through her; she remembered the words which she had spoken: "the wish for the best for herself and Rudy."

"Woe is me! Was that the sinful seed in my heart? Did my dream foretell my future life? Is all this misery for my salvation? Me, miserable one!"

Lamenting, sat she in the dark night. In the solemn stillness, sounded Rudy's last words; the last ones he had uttered: "Earth has no more happiness to give me!" She had heard it in the fullness of her joy, she heard it again in all the depths of her sorrow.

A couple of years have passed since then. The lake smiles, the coast smiles; the vine branches are filled with ripe grapes; the steamboats glide along with waving flags and the pleasure boats float over the watery mirror, with their two expanded sails like white butterflies. The railroad to Chillon is opened; it leads into the Rhone valley; strangers alight at every station; they arrive with their red covered guide books and read of remarkable sights which are to be seen.

They visit Chillon, they stand upon the little island, with its three acacias—out on the lake—and they read in the book about the betrothed ones, who sailed over one evening in the year 1856;—of the death of the bridegroom, and: "it was not till the next morning, that the despairing shrieks of the bride were heard on the coast!"

The book does not tell, however, of Babette's quiet life with her father; not in the mill, where strangers now dwell, but in the beautiful house, near the railway station. There she looks from the window many an evening and gazes over the chestnut trees, upon the snow mountains, where Rudy once climbed. She sees in the evening hours the alpine glow—the children of the Sun encamp themselves above, and repeat the song of the wanderer, whose mantle the whirlwind tore off, and carried away: "it took the covering but not the man."

There is a rosy hue on the snow of the mountains; there is a rosy hue in every heart, where the thought dwells, that: "God always gives us that which is best for us!" but it is not always revealed to us, as it once happened to Babette in her dream.

The Little Match Girl

It was dreadfully cold; it was snowing fast, and was almost dark, as evening came on—the last evening of the year. In the cold and the darkness, there went along the street a poor little girl, bareheaded and with naked feet. When she left home she had slippers on, it is true; but they were much too large for her feet—slippers that her mother had used till then, and the poor little girl lost them in running across the street when two carriages were passing terribly fast. When she looked for them, one was not to be found, and a boy seized the other and ran away with it, saying he would use it for a cradle some day, when he had children of his own.

So on the little girl went with her bare feet, that were red and blue with cold. In an old apron that she wore were bundles of matches, and she carried a bundle also in her hand. No one had bought so much as a bunch all the long day, and no one had given her even a penny.

Poor little girl! Shivering with cold and hunger she crept along, a perfect picture of misery.

The snowflakes fell on her long flaxen hair, which hung in pretty curls about her throat; but she thought not of her beauty nor of the cold. Lights gleamed in every window, and there came to her the savory smell of roast goose, for it was New Year's Eve. And it was this of which she thought.

In a corner formed by two houses, one of which projected beyond the other, she sat cowering down. She had drawn under her her little feet, but still she grew colder and colder; yet she dared not go home, for she had sold no matches and could not bring a penny of money. Her father would certainly beat her; and, besides, it was cold enough at home, for they had only the house-roof above them, and though the largest holes had been stopped with straw and rags, there were left many through which the cold wind could whistle.

And now her little hands were nearly frozen with cold. Alas! a single match might do her good if she might only draw it from the bundle, rub it against the wall, and warm her fingers by it. So at last she drew one out. Whisht! How it blazed and burned! It gave out a warm, bright flame like a little candle, as she held her hands over it.

A wonderful little light it was. It really seemed to the little girl as if she sat before a great iron stove with polished brass feet and brass shovel and tongs. So blessedly it burned that the little maiden stretched out her feet to warm them also. How comfortable she was! But lo! the flame went out, the stove vanished, and nothing remained but the little burned match in her hand.

She rubbed another match against the wall. It burned brightly, and where the light fell upon the wall it became transparent like a veil, so that she could see through it into the room. A snow-white cloth was spread upon the table, on which was a beautiful china dinner-service, while a roast goose, stuffed with apples and prunes, steamed famously and sent forth a most savory smell.

And what was more delightful still, and wonderful, the goose jumped from the dish, with knife and fork still in its breast, and waddled along the floor straight to the little girl.

But the match went out then, and nothing was left to her but the thick, damp wall.

She lighted another match. And now she was under a most beautiful Christmas tree, larger and far more prettily trimmed than the one she had seen through the glass doors at the rich merchant's. Hundreds of wax tapers were burning on the green branches, and gay figures, such as she had seen in shop windows, looked down upon her. The child stretched out her hands to them; then the match went out.

Still the lights of the Christmas tree rose higher and higher. She saw them now as stars in heaven, and one of them fell, forming a long trail of fire.

"Now some one is dying," murmured the child softly; for her grandmother, the only person who had loved her, and who was now dead, had told her that whenever a star falls a soul mounts up to God.

She struck yet another match against the wall, and again it was light; and in the brightness there appeared before her the dear old grandmother, bright and radiant, yet sweet and mild, and happy as she had never looked on earth.

"Oh, grandmother," cried the child, "take me with you. I know you will go away when the match burns out. You, too, will vanish, like the warm stove, the splendid New Year's feast, the beautiful Christmas tree." And lest her grandmother should disappear, she rubbed the whole bundle of matches against the wall.

And the matches burned with such a brilliant light that it became brighter than noonday. Her grandmother had never looked so grand and beautiful. She took the little girl in her arms, and both flew together, joyously and gloriously, mounting higher and higher, far above the earth; and for them there was neither hunger, nor cold, nor care—they were with God.

But in the corner, at the dawn of day, sat the poor girl, leaning against the wall, with red cheeks and smiling mouth—
frozen to death on the last evening of the old year. Stiff and
cold she sat, with the matches, one bundle of which was
burned.

"She wanted to warm herself, poor little thing," people said.
No one imagined what sweet visions she had had, or how
gloriously she had gone with her grandmother to enter upon
the joys of a new year.

The Red Shoes

There was once a pretty, delicate little girl, who was so poor that she had to go barefoot in summer and wear coarse wooden shoes in winter, which made her little instep quite red.

In the center of the village there lived an old shoemaker's wife. One day this good woman made, as well as she could, a little pair of shoes out of some strips of old red cloth. The shoes were clumsy enough, to be sure, but they fitted the little girl tolerably well, and anyway the woman's intention was kind. The little girl's name was Karen.

On the very day that Karen received the shoes, her mother was to be buried. They were not at all suitable for mourning, but she had no others,

so she put them on her little bare feet and followed the poor plain coffin to its last resting place.

Just at that time a large, old-fashioned carriage happened to pass by, and the old lady who sat in it saw the little girl and pitied her.

"Give me the little girl," she said to the clergyman, "and I will take care of her."

Karen supposed that all this happened because of the red shoes, but the old lady thought them frightful and ordered them to be burned. Karen was then dressed in neat, well-fitting clothes and taught to read and sew. People told her she was pretty, but the mirror said, "You are much more than pretty—you are beautiful."

It happened not long afterwards that the queen and her little daughter, the princess, traveled through the land.

All the people, Karen among the rest, flocked toward the palace and crowded around it, while the little princess, dressed in white, stood at the window for every one to see. She wore neither a train nor a golden crown, but on her feet were beautiful red morocco shoes, which, it must be admitted, were prettier than those the shoemaker's wife had given to little Karen. Surely nothing in the world could be compared to those red shoes.

Now that Karen was old enough to be confirmed, she of course had to have a new frock and new shoes. The rich shoemaker in the town took the measure of her little feet in his own house, in a room where stood great glass cases filled with all sorts of fine shoes and elegant, shining boots.

It was a pretty sight, but the old lady could not see well and naturally did not take so much pleasure in it as Karen. Among the shoes were a pair of red ones, just like those worn by the little princess. Oh, how gay they were! The shoemaker said they had been made for the child of a count, but had not fitted well.

"Are they of polished leather, that they shine so?" asked the old lady.

"Yes, indeed, they do shine," replied Karen. And since they fitted her, they were bought. But the old lady had no idea that they were red, or she would never in the world have allowed Karen to go to confirmation in them, as she now did. Every one, of course, looked at Karen's shoes; and when she walked up the nave to the chancel it seemed to her that even the antique figures on the monuments, the portraits of clergymen and their wives, with their stiff ruffs and long black robes, were fixing their eyes on her red shoes.

Even when the bishop laid his hand upon her head and spoke of her covenant with God and how she must now begin to be a full-grown Christian, and when the organ pealed forth solemnly and the children's fresh, sweet voices joined with those of the choir—still Karen thought of nothing but her shoes.

In the afternoon, when the old lady heard every one speak of the red shoes, she said it was very shocking and improper and that, in the future, when Karen went to church it must always be in black shoes, even if they were old.

The next Sunday was Karen's first Communion day. She looked at her black shoes, and then at her red ones, then again at the black and at the red—and the red ones were put on.

The sun shone very brightly, and Karen and the old lady walked to church through the cornfields, for the road was very dusty.

At the door of the church stood an old soldier, who leaned upon a crutch and had a marvelously long beard that was not white but red. He bowed almost to the ground and asked the old lady if he might dust her shoes. Karen, in her turn, put out her little foot.

"Oh, look, what smart little dancing pumps!" said the old soldier. "Mind you do not let them slip off when you dance," and he passed his hands over them. The old lady gave the soldier a half-penny and went with Karen into the church.

As before, every one saw Karen's red shoes, and all the carved figures too bent their gaze upon them. When Karen knelt at the chancel she thought only of the shoes; they floated before her eyes, and she forgot to say her prayer or sing her psalm.

At last all the people left the church, and the old lady got into her carriage. As Karen lifted her foot to step in, the old soldier said, "See what pretty dancing shoes!" And Karen, in spite of herself, made a few dancing steps. When she had once begun, her feet went on of themselves; it was as though the shoes had received power over her.

She danced round the church corner,—she could not help it, —and the coachman had to run behind and catch her to put her into the carriage. Still her feet went on dancing, so, that she trod upon the good lady's toes. It was not until the shoes were taken from her feet that she had rest.

The shoes were put away in a closet, but Karen could not resist going to look at them every now and then.

Soon after this the old lady lay ill in bed, and it was said that she could not recover. She had to be nursed and waited on, and this, of course, was no one's duty so much as it was Karen's, as Karen herself well knew. But there happened to be a great ball in the town, and Karen was invited. She looked at the old lady, who was very ill, and she looked at the red shoes. She put them on, for she thought there could not be any sin in that, and of course there was not—but she went next to the ball and began to dance.

Strange to say, when she wanted to move to the right the shoes bore her to the left; and when she wished to dance up the room the shoes persisted in going down the room. Down the stairs they carried her at last, into the street, and out through the town gate. On and on she danced, for dance she must, straight out into the gloomy wood. Up among the trees something glistened. She thought it was the round, red moon, for she saw a face; but no, it was the old soldier with the red beard, who sat and nodded, saying, "See what pretty dancing shoes!"

She was dreadfully frightened and tried to throw away the red shoes, but they clung fast and she could not unclasp them. They seemed to have grown fast to her feet. So dance she must, and dance she did, over field and meadow, in rain and in sunshine, by night and by day—and by night it was by far more dreadful.

She danced out into the open churchyard, but the dead there did not dance; they were at rest and had much better things to do. She would have liked to sit down on the poor man's grave, where the bitter tansy grew, but for her there was no rest.

She danced past the open church door, and there she saw an angel in long white robes and with wings that reached from his shoulders to

the earth. His look was stern and grave, and in his hand he held a broad, glittering sword.

"Thou shalt dance," he said, "in thy red shoes, till thou art pale and cold, and till thy body is wasted like a skeleton. Thou shalt dance from door to door, and wherever proud, haughty children dwell thou shalt knock, that, hearing thee, they may take warning. Dance thou shalt—dance on!"

"Mercy!" cried Karen; but she did not hear the answer of the angel, for the shoes carried her past the door and on into the fields.

One morning she danced past a well-known door. Within was the sound of a psalm, and presently a coffin strewn with flowers was borne out. She knew that her friend, the old lady, was dead, and in her heart she felt that she was abandoned by all on earth and condemned by God's angel in heaven.

Still on she danced—for she could not stop—through thorns and briers, while her feet bled. Finally, she danced to a lonely little house where she knew that the executioner dwelt, and she tapped at the window, saying, "Come out, come out! I cannot come in, for I must dance."

The man said, "Do you know who I am and what I do?"

"Yes," said Karen; "but do not strike off my head, for then I could not live to repent of my sin. Strike off my feet, that I may be rid of my red shoes."

Then she confessed her sin, and the executioner struck off the red shoes, which danced away over the fields and into the deep wood. To Karen it seemed that the feet had gone with the shoes, for she had almost lost the power of walking.

"Now I have suffered enough for the red shoes," she said; "I will go to the church, that people may see me." But no sooner had she hobbled to the church door than the shoes danced before her and frightened her back.

All that week she endured the keenest sorrow and shed many bitter tears. When Sunday came, she said: "I am sure I must have suffered and striven enough by this time. I am quite as good, I dare say, as many who are holding their heads high in the church." So she took courage and went again. But before she reached the churchyard gate the red shoes were dancing there, and she turned back again in terror, more deeply sorrowful than ever for her sin.

She then went to the pastor's house and begged as a favor to be taken into the family's service, promising to be diligent and faithful. She did not want wages, she said, only a home with good people. The clergyman's wife pitied her and granted her request, and she proved industrious and very thoughtful.

Earnestly she listened when at evening the preacher read aloud the Holy Scriptures. All the children came to love her, but when they spoke of beauty and finery, she would shake her head and turn away.

On Sunday, when they all went to church, they asked her if she would not go, too, but she looked sad and bade them go without her. Then she went to her own little room, and as she sat with the psalm book in her hand, reading its pages with a gentle, pious mind, the wind brought to her the notes of the organ. She raised her tearful eyes and said, "O God, do thou help me!"

Then the sun shone brightly, and before her stood the white angel that she had seen at the church door. He no longer bore the glittering sword, but in his hand was a beautiful branch of roses. He touched the ceiling with it, and the ceiling rose, and at each place where the branch touched it there shone a star. He touched the walls, and they widened so that Karen could see the organ that was being played at the church.

She saw, too, the old pictures and statues on the walls, and the congregation sitting in the seats and singing psalms, for the church itself had come to the poor girl in her narrow room, or she in her chamber had come to it. She sat in the seat with the rest of the clergyman's household, and when the psalm was ended, they nodded and said, "Thou didst well to come, Karen!"

"This is mercy," said she. "It is the grace of God."

The organ pealed, and the chorus of children's voices mingled sweetly with it. The bright sunshine shed its warm light, through the windows, over the pew in which Karen sat. Her heart was so filled with sunshine, peace, and joy that it broke, and her soul was borne by a sunbeam up to God, where there was nobody to ask about the red shoes.

Printed in Great Britain
by Amazon

45060658R00092